Every Time I Close My Eyes

Taya R. Hargrove

Regal Publishing, Inc.,
2 Burbank Blvd
Savannah, Georgia 31419
www.regalpublishing.com

Printed in the United States of America

Copyright © 2002 by Taya R. Hargrove

Library of Congress Control Number: 2002095907

ISBN 0-9717355-2-2

REGAL PAPERBACK FICTION
PUBLISHED BY REGAL PUBLISHING, INC.
UNITED STATES OF AMERICA

Visit our Web site at http:// www.regalpublishing.com

Praise for Every Time I Close My Eyes:

"As an avid reader, I found Taya Hargrove's literary debut refreshing. Her characters were easy to visualize and the story flowed. I look forward to her future works!"

~Gayle W. Bowens
Governor's Office of Georgia

"Every Time I Close My Eyes is incredibly engaging and grabs your attention from the beginning! Through Shelby, Taya Hargrove has brought to life the complex emotions of anyone, regardless of gender or race that has ever been involved with someone they believed was too good to be true. I was instantly drawn to the courage and vulnerability of Shelby."

~Imani Turner-Barrett
English Teacher (Adult Education)
Dekalb Trauncy School

"Every Time I Close My Eyes is a beautiful story! Taya Hargrove writes with such detail that I felt as though I was witnessing the story first hand!"

~Cleshia Sledge

"This book was so riveting that I didn't want to put it down."

~Nancy Alston
Executive Assistant, Sperion

"A captivating 'cannot' put down book. I was hooked from page one!"

~Vincent Seals

"This is a wonderful debut novel for Taya Hargrove. It symbolizes how focused women have become, particularly after a divorce or ended relationship and defines how we must regroup and continue to set high standards."

~Angela Sellers-Mann
6th Grade Teacher, Freedom Middle School

"I have a very vivid imagination. This novel is so well written and descriptive that I could visualize the story as clearly as if I were watching television. I really enjoyed this book!"

~Brinda J. Morrow

Acknowledgments

Thanks to one of my dearest friends, Doretha Jackson, who asked for new chapters faster then I could write them. You helped bring this story to life by convincing me that maybe I could write a book. Thanks Doe! Thanks to my other "bestest" Cassandra Myers for being such an encouraging spiritual sister, for laughing with me, crying with me, and sitting quietly with me, and for always letting me say what I need to say -- and then correcting me (I still mean what I said about paradise). Feicia Edwards, you have very broad shoulders for a spiritual sister of such petite stature. Thank you for being there since way back when (you know when I'm talking about). Mara Lee Mims, you are such a good example and such a strong spiritual (big) sister, thank you for being you.

I also want to thank my family - The Bakers. Growing up as the oldest and only girl in a house full of boys made my creative imagination kick in very early. Thank you to my husband, Freddie L. Hargrove, Jr., for your patience with me. You think I'm a little "off center," but you know I always make you smile. Leo Sullivan thanks for encouraging my writing and forever trying to tell me how to do it (I wish you the best in your writing endeavors). Karen Trower, Jacquie Reeves, Michelle Lester, and Cathy Tiggs thanks for all the love throughout the years. I also want to thank all of my friends and co-workers who have either listened to me talk about my book or have read it, or parts thereof, at one time or another (asking for updates throughout the years, motivated me to continue). Denise Bryant, thank you for convincing me to talk about it...put it out there...make it real...obligate myself to it (boy am I obligated now). Gayle Bowens thanks for that phone call girl! Evelyn Armour thanks to "you" for having such ambitious and industrious friends.

Finally, thanks to my publisher, Regal Publishing, Inc., and James Jackson for making me believe that writing might possibly prove to be more then just something that I do in my spare time.

Prologue

It is July 31, 1995 and I'm sitting here wondering, when people think about getting married, do they consider that one day it might end in divorce? I know I didn't. I used to think that getting a divorce would be the worst thing in the world that could possibly happen to me, but I've since learned that it's not! I always thought I would be devastated if I had to go through it, but I'm not. I don't think there's anything wrong with treating myself to a couple of drinks and a little dinner because my divorce finalized today. I haven't had any White Zinfandel in a long time or the opportunity to enjoy a romantic dinner. Heaven knows my husband never took me anywhere. But hey, I'm not going to go there.

I hadn't seen my waiter in a while, so I looked around the restaurant and there he was, this absolutely gorgeous man! I wondered who he was because he looked kind of important. He was tall, had a mustache, a neatly trimmed haircut, and he was dressed very casually. He had a beautiful smile and a glow to his skin that led me to believe that he smelled good. With broad shoulders and a tapered waistline, he had the appearance of a professional athlete or some celebrity that I'd seen before. I was lost in thought, so by the time I realized that he was looking at me I couldn't break my gaze. Good for me that I was having one of my really cute days. Sometimes 5'9", pecan shell brown, slim sisters with mid-length hair, deserve to get checked out too. So, I kept looking at the tall, handsome stranger until "I" got tired! I didn't think there was any harm in that. Was there?

Well, I've had enough wine and salad. I don't know what the hold up is with my food. I wish they would hurry up before that guy comes over here and says something to me. You know, you can't look at a man without him thinking that you want him! Men are so full of themselves! I thought I saw my waiter, but if the food he was carrying wasn'tmine I was going to have to leave and stop at Burger King on the way home.

About the Author

Taya R. Hargrove is a graduate of Florida State University in Tallahassee, Florida, and has a B.S. in Criminal Justice and Psychology. She currently resides in Stone Mountain, Georgia, and works in the Office of the Governor as the Extradition Coordinator for the State of Georgia. Ms. Hargrove is currently working on a book of poetry and her second and third novels.

CHAPTER

1

*L*ook at this I knew I should have stopped looking at him.

"Hi, a few minutes ago you were staring and I thought maybe you were flirting with me."

I looked up at him and casually said, "I wasn't flirting with you. I was looking "at" you! I apologize for being rude, but you're a very attractive man."

He smiled (and his smile was absolutely beautiful) as he extended his hand, "I guess I should introduce myself. My name is Julian and I am very flattered that you find me attractive. I have to tell you that I'm a little surprised by your boldness."

I slowly extended my hand and introduced myself. I thought this was the proper thing to do.

"Hi Julian, my name is Shelby. It's a pleasure to make your acquaintance. I really didn't mean to disturb you. I apologize. You shouldn't have had to leave your dinner party to come over here." To my surprise he told me that it was no problem and he asked if he could join me. I told him that it was okay, so he went over to his table, grabbed his food, and came back. Can you believe it? "So Shelby, why were you flirting with me? Your boyfriend could have walked in and misunderstood what was happening?" I couldn't help but smile because deep down inside I was flirting, but I never intended to get more then a smile back from him. "I don't think my boyfriend would have gotten the wrong impression, I'm single. Anyway, I was just looking, that's all! Like I said before, I think you're very attractive." We finally got past the flirting dialogue and started talking about other things. He wanted to know why I was there alone. I wanted to know why he was there with so many people. We did what seemed like normal chitchat and before we knew it we had talked for about three hours. His entourage was ready to go and I really had to leave too because life had not stopped because of the divorce. Julian asked for my phone number, so I gave him my business card and we bid our farewells. I told him that I had enjoyed dinner and that the company and the conversation had been very pleasant and then he asked me "the" question. "When can I see you again?" I really didn't want to start anything that I couldn't finish and I didn't want to lead him on. There was really no point in seeing him again (no matter how fine he was). What did I look like starting a new relationship on the very day that my divorce became final? "I'll tell you what. I don't work too far away, so I'll stop by here one day next week. Let's just say that we'll see each other the next time we're both here."

He wasn't upset by my response, but he did want to know why I wouldn't set a date and a time to meet him. I ignored his question and explained that I wasn't sure which evening I would be there, but I did know that it would probably be a Wednesday or a Friday. So that was that! We shook hands, he left with his friends and I left with my pleasant memories of the evening.

Well, the next week could not come fast enough. I stopped by the restaurant on Wednesday evening and guess who was already there... Julian was sitting at a nice secluded booth and he had a single pink rose with him. That boy looked just as good as he did the first time I saw him. He stood up as I approached him. I just couldn't get over how good he looked. He always looked like he was going to smile at any minute. Anyway, we spoke, he handed me the rose, and we sat down. I had to order a glass of wine to relax. Although I'm sure I looked calm, I wasn't.

"Well, good evening. Thank you for the rose," I said.

"It's going to be a good evening now! I was afraid that you were going to make me wait until Friday to see you."

I smiled when he said that. It never crossed my mind to wait until Friday.

Dinner was great, the conversation was fantastic, and his company was even better the second time around. We spent most of the evening talking about his singing career. You know, it's kind of funny because I knew he looked like somebody I had seen before. I just couldn't put my finger on it. He was Jules Brishard, the R&B singer. I'm slow, but I usually figure things out. His career was just picking up and he was starting to do more interviews and even had his concert schedule lined up. He had been trying to break into the music business for about eight years and all of his hard work and discipline was finally starting to pay off. I thought it was pretty interesting that he was an "entertainer type." He seemed too mellow and down to earth. For some reason I assumed that all entertainers were arrogant and high strung! Shows how much I know.

We talked about my marriage and what had gone wrong in it. I didn't go into great detail because I didn't think that would be fair to my ex. He wasn't around to defend himself or to tell his version of the story. I was very general about most things that we discussed and of course there were some things that I didn't even bother mentioning. We talked about the kind of personalities that we were attracted to and people that we had dated. He said he was impressed by my candor and the kind of person that I appeared to be. I didn't say anything, but I was impressed with him too. He was very down to earth and easy to talk too. I liked that.

CHAPTER
2

$\mathcal{W}$e continued to meet once a week, for what seemed like forever, but it was only about two months. The weeks that we didn't see each other, we made sure that we talked. Julian would call me once or twice during the week or I would call him once or twice. One day as I was sitting at a table in "our" restaurant, waiting for Julian to get there, a young lady (I'd say early twenties) walked over to the table.

"Are you waiting on Jules Brishard?"

My first thought was, "Is this a groupie or is she going to threaten me and tell me she's Julian's baby's mama?"

I answered her by playing ignorant, "Excuse me? Is there a problem?"

She was very nice as she told me, "There is no real problem, but I know someone who would not appreciate you having dinner with him. So maybe you should consider not meeting him anymore!"

I smiled and said, "I see."

Then she just walked away? It was weird. Actually, the more I thought about it, the more I thought that she was probably a groupie. She didn't appear to be the kind of person that Julian would date anyway. She looked to young to travel in the circles that he traveled in. I got the impression that he liked his women a little more mature then she appeared. I don't know...being approached by the young lady didn't bother me, that much, but I did think Julian should know about it.

When he arrived he apologized for being late, said he got held up at the studio in some sort of meeting or something. He walked over to me and kissed me on the cheek! This was definitely a new stage in our relationship because he had never even motioned to kiss me before that day! From behind his back he handed me an oblong gift box and said, "Happy anniversary!" I was really impressed because it had been exactly two months since we met. Even though I had gotten him a card, I didn't think that was the sort of information that a man would keep up with. I handed him his card and said, "Happy anniversary to you too!" I opened my gift. It was a very delicate, serpentine, silver chain with a beautiful princess cut diamond pendant hanging from it. This man was too much! I said thank you and asked him why he would buy something so expensive for me. He said the money was irrelevant and that he wanted me to have something nice.

"I thought I might scare you away if I bought the ring too soon."

Okay, so I was speechless. What do you say to the "faunest" man in town when he, in so many words, tells you that he wants to someday marry you?

He proceeded to get up and walk around my chair, so that he could help me put my necklace on. I guess there was nothing else to be said about the necklace...or the ring? He asked me if it was okay if he read the card when he got home? I thought it a bit strange and I was a little disappointed that I wouldn't see his reaction when he read it, but that was okay, I didn't mind too much...

I finally broke down and told him what the young lady told me earlier. We discussed it, and he assured me that he wasn't seeing anyone else. He was very, very adamant about it, and a little angry. He didn't know why someone would stoop so low and say that to me, but he suggested that next time we should meet at his house. He thought that would be a little safer, since the young lady really could have been some kind of psycho or something. Apprehensively, I agreed to meet him at his house for our next tête-à-tête.

Julian's house was far more beautiful than I had ever imagined. I pulled up in front of a huge, beige, stucco mansion. I could not believe my eyes as I was driving onto the two lane circular drive. It was just like him not to tell me that he lived so grandiosely. As a matter of fact, he never talked about his money or the things that he had acquired with his newfound wealth, and I never asked. I knew that I was at the right house, but I thought that maybe I had the days mixed up because there were six or seven cars in the driveway. I almost decided not to stop, but I thought since

I had driven this far I might as well go all the way. I got out of my car and went up to the door. I hardly got one good ring from the doorbell when Julian opened the door. He said he had been looking out for me because he thought I might get lost. As I walked in he grabbed me by my left hand, kissed me on my left cheek and closed the door as we said our hello's. I told him that I almost kept driving because there were so many cars in the driveway. I thought that maybe he had invited a few of his friends over to hang out. After noticing all of the people inside, I looked at him and thought I must have my days mixed up? He explained that he thought I would feel more comfortable if I wasn't there with him alone, he had invited a few people over to hang out. I looked at him and thought how sweet and thoughtful that was...we had chaperones.

Julian introduced me to everyone and they all seemed to be pretty nice folks. Then we had a really, really nice evening! We sat by the pool and had dinner by candlelight. I took this time to tell Julian that I thought of him as a very good friend. He didn't like that.

"Julian, I think that you are absolutely wonderful, but I'm not ready for a relationship yet. I think we have a really good friendship going."

Julian looked at me like I was crazy, "So, when can we become more then friends? Is there anything that I can do to change your mind?"

"Right now I just don't have the mind set to date. Anyway, things get so complicated, sex and everything, you know? And we're not even going to go there because I'm just not going to have sex with anyone that I'm not married to.

There was no room for discussion when it came to that subject. I think Julian was a little disappointed, but it was hard to tell. He had a really sweet, little boy look on his face as he listened to me.

"I understand."

And that was the end of that portion of our conversation.

We continued to talk into the night. Julian mentioned several parties that would take place in the next few months. He wanted me to attend them with him. I'm not a party person, so I wouldn't be going to a lot of them. I really wasn't "into" parties where there might be a lot of drugging, drinking, and stuff going on. Julian laughed at me and said I read too many tabloids. All entertainers didn't drink and do drugs. I guess he had a point there. Nevertheless, he was very understanding again and told me that it was okay. More then anything he just wanted to spend time with me. He felt that, maybe, in time, one thing or the other would change, but in the mean time he hoped we could continue to hang out together.

Julian pleaded with me to go to one party with him and he gave me his word that he wouldn't make a habit of asking me to attend too many functions. I agreed to go and even agreed to let him buy me a dress. We made plans to go shopping on Sunday, which was two days away. I realized it was getting late (really late, 2:00am) and most of Julian's houseguests had left so, I thought I'd better get myself on home. Being the gentlemen that he is, Julian offered me a room for the night (not his of course), but I didn't think it would be prudent to accept his invitation.

As I drove home I thought about how compatible Julian and I seemed to be and how we always had something to talk about, even if it was trivial. I chuckled out loud when I thought about how comfortable I felt with him. It was as though I had known him for years, instead of just a few months. I came to the unwavering conclusion that we had to be soul mates. I knew that he wanted to be more than platonic friends and whether I wanted to admit it or not, I wanted him to be more then just a friend too. I did a lot of praying because I didn't want to put myself into any compromising situations with Julian or lead him on, but at the same time I really did enjoy being with him.

CHAPTER

3

*S*aturday evening my phone rang and it was Julian. He told me he had a surprise for me, but I had to be at his house before sunset. I didn't have anything planned, so I agreed to meet him at his house around 7:30pm. When I arrived he was waiting outside. I got out of my car and he ushered me into his. We rode down to the beach. Once we arrived he spread a blanket over the sand. He then went back to the car and pulled a wicker picnic basket from the trunk. I sat on the blanket thinking, "I can not believe this man! Did he not hear anything that I said to him last night?" I wasn't upset though, it had been a long time since I'd been romanced by a man. We were both going to get in over our heads if he kept doing things like this. He pulled fruit, cheese, crackers, a portable CD player, two wineglasses, and a bottle of wine out of the basket.

After pouring two glasses of wine, Julian held my hand. "I heard everything you said last night, but girl I can't get you off my mind. I appreciate your frankness with me because I'm not used to that. This might sound like a line, but you're not like anyone else that I've ever met."

I attempted to interrupt him, but he pressed his fingers

against my lips.

"We've only known each other for a short time, but I feel like I've known you for years. And you know what's strange? I think I'm falling in love with you. I'm not asking you for anything and I'm not trying to put any pressure on you or anything like that."

I sat there silently, in shock, wondering where all of this was coming from?

He then said, "Just let me share the sunsets with you from time to time."

Then he turned away, took a drink from his glass, and looked at the ocean as I sat looking at him totally dumbfounded. I didn't know what was more beautiful, him or the sunset. His words kept playing through my mind, "I think I'm falling in love with you..." Just when I thought my heart couldn't take anymore I felt Julian's hand on my cheek. He turned my face toward his and he gently kissed me. It was awesome! Everything about this man was unbelievable! Those few moments seemed surreal sort of like it was all happening in slow motion. For a brief moment he stopped kissing me and sat back. We looked at each other and then we kissed again. I thought the second kiss was going to last forever (sort of cliché, but that's how it felt). I didn't want it to end. His kiss was the strongest, softest, sweetest kiss that I had ever had in my life. When it was over neither one of us said a word, we just turned away and watched the sunset.

It seemed like all I waited for was the next time I would see Julian. I was going to work every day, spending time with my friends, and going on with my day-to-day life, but Julian was always on my mind! I wondered what he was doing, if he was thinking about me, what he was wearing? You know...silly stuff! It was hard to believe that almost three months had gone by and I hadn't told any of my friends or family about him. It wasn't that I was keeping him a secret. I just wasn't quite ready to share him with anyone else just yet. Another strange thing was that he had never been to my condo. That was going to change because he was going to pick me up for the party this weekend. We always spent time at his house or other places, so there was really no need for him to come to my place. I didn't mind either way.

I was trying real hard to keep things in perspective. After all, I was the one that said we were just going to be friends and that our relationship would probably never go beyond that. If I really believed what I was saying, I wouldn't be thinking about him all the time. One day I even thought, if I didn't know any better I'd think I was falling in love with that boy. When I'm with him I feel good about myself. He doesn't make any unreasonable demands of me. He lets me do what ever I deem will make him happy (that was always a problem with my ex-husband) and we can talk about anything. He's not pretentious. He's warm, generous, caring, and giving. You know...all of the good things. As much as I wanted to control my feelings, I couldn't and I'm sure Julian knew that. I'm certain he knew the effect he had on me and he didn't seem to have a problem expressing himself. Unlike my ex when we were dating, it never once crossed my mind that Julian was "too good to be true." I couldn't even imagine him being anything other then what he is. Enough, enough, enough, I could go on talking about him forever!

Well, party night finally came and I looked absolutely gorgeous in the dress that Julian and I picked out together. It was purple and fuchsia and the hem stopped just a little above the knee. It had a sheer overlay with gold specks on it. It wasn't a spaghetti strapped dress, but it was sleeveless. My shoes were purple pumps with gold and purple on the toe. I wore my hair pulled up and the earrings that I wore were gold. When I looked at myself in the mirror I thought, he's going to like this! Before I could finish admiring myself the doorbell rang. I immediately became nervous, like it was our first date or something. Actually it was, we had never attended any parties or visited other people while we were together. We had been spending all of our time together alone. This would be our coming out date.

When I opened the door, we both stood there looking at each other from head to toe. He was absolutely gorgeous in his black tux. His cummerbund and tie were purple, fuchsia, blue, and gold. For a minute I almost forgot to ask him

in. When I came back to my senses I was able to speak.
"Well, Julian Brishard, come in!"

When he stepped into the foyer he grabbed me by my
waist, pulled me close to him and kissed me. It was just like
the very first time we kissed, strong and sweet. Actually,
every kiss was just like the very first kiss.

Then he said, "Step back and let me look at you. You
look so good I could stay here all night just looking at you.
Somebody might try to steal you from me tonight."

Then he smiled, like he does, and I had to ask God to
please help me maintain myself.

The ride to the party in the white super stretch limousine was really nice. I had a glass of wine on the way. We
spent most of the ride holding hands and looking at each
other (corny I know...) and to be perfectly honest with you,
I wouldn't have had a problem with missing the party all
together. I was perfectly content riding around town in the
back seat of a limousine with Julian. When we arrived at the
party limousines were everywhere. I felt a little anxious and
wondered if I had made the right decision. I hoped there
wouldn't be a lot of craziness going on. The house was
located on the top of a hill, part of which hung over a cliff.
It was white stucco and windows were everywhere.

Before we stepped in, Julian looked at me and asked,
"Are you ready?"

So I asked, "Ready for what?"

"Everybody's going to be checking you out ... because
you're gorgeous and because you're with me. There might

be a few jealous women here too, but don't worry, nothing foolish is going to happen. I'm going to be with you at all times. Just be prepared because you're definitely going to be the center of attention."

So I said, "Okay, let's go..."

When we walked through the door it was just like Julian said it was going to be. It seemed like everything, except the music, stopped and all eyes were on us. Or should I say, on me. I could see some people smiling, some whispering, some nudging each other. Then there were a few women who just kind of glared at me, as if to say, "Who do you think you are coming here with him?" Obviously all of the attention didn't phase Julian one bit. He immediately began introducing me to people. It appeared that I was very well received, for the most part. Julian got me a glass of wine and told me to relax. While we were standing there Julian pointed out people that he thought I would recognize and every now and then he would say something funny about somebody. He also pointed out two women, one he had previously dated for a while and the other he had gone out with a couple of times. He felt the need to assure me that they were history long before he ever met me. No explanation was needed. I didn't feel threatened. I was at the party with him ... and they weren't! While we were standing there laughing two record producers walked up and asked me if they could steal Julian away for a few minutes. He excused himself, kissed me on the cheek, and said he'd be right back.

It seemed like Julian had been gone for hours, even though it had only been about three or four minutes. It was at this time that I had the pleasure of meeting "Smokie." I later learned that Smokie was Julian's best friend. I was surprised that I hadn't heard of him or met him sooner at Julian's house, but of course I had not met a lot of Julian's friends.

Smokie walked up to me and whispered in my ear, "You look incredible! I didn't see you come in with anybody, so it would be my pleasure if you'd be my date for the rest of the night. How would you feel about leaving here and going some place where we could talk and have a couple of drinks?"

I looked at him and said, "Do I know you? Thanks for the invitation, but I have to decline."

Smokie appeared to be a "funny kind of guy" (one with a good sense of humor that is...). He was very handsome, with smooth black skin (flawless) and he came across as kind of persistent, but comical. His advances didn't offend me at all, but there was something about him that rubbed me the wrong way (at the time I couldn't figure it out...). Smokie kept insisting that I leave with him. He said I was too fine to be standing by myself at any party. I finally told him that I came with Julian Brishard and that I was his new secretary.

He chuckled a little bit and said, "Well go 'head Julian! I didn't think he had it in him! I thought everybody he hired to work for him was over 50."

I had no idea what he meant by that, but without missing a beat Smokie told me that Julian very seldom came to parties with a date, that was, when he even bothered to come at all.

"You must give good shorthand! Julian doesn't kick it with just anybody or haven't you been around long enough to know that?"

I didn't respond. I just stood there looking at him. I finally asked, "Do you know Julian very well? From what I've seen so far, he seems to be a pretty laid back guy. Am I right?"

"Very good guess. For guessing correctly you can have a drink with me at my favorite joint."

Just as I was about to say no thank you again, Julian walked up. He apologized for being away so long and then turned to Smokie. "Man, I see you've met Shelby. I hope you weren't sweatin' her? Shelby, this is my best friend Smokie."

Smokie smiled, "Man, you know me! So this is the friend you were trying to tell me about. It was nice meeting you Shelby. I'm sure I'll see you again soon."

Julian and I held hands as we walked to the patio. We sat and talked until I finally told him that I was too tired to hang out anymore. Parties just weren't my thing, and I had made my appearance. I told Julian that if he wasn't ready to go that was okay, he could stay. He talked me into staying just a little while longer, so he could rub a few more elbows (and show me off some more). We ended up dancing and talking to the hosts for another two hours.

As we left the house to walk to the car I could see Smokie watching us from across the room. I had a real strange feeling about him, but I just couldn't put my finger on it. I made sure that I said good-bye to the hosts. I thanked them for having such a "lovely" party, assured them that Julian and I would have dinner with them soon, and apologized for leaving so early. Once we made our way out to the car, Julian gave me a nice long kiss. As I looked at him I thought, please don't have multiple personalities, or do drugs, or be a criminal. Please be for real! I took my right hand and gently grabbed his face and kissed him again.

"Thank you for tonight, I had a nice time."

As he closed the door, he smiled and said, "Thanks for coming."

On the ride home I felt like a princess. I hoped our relationship wasn't too good to be true. I'm tired of the story ending that way. I want him to be "THE ONE!" I was already in over my head. Now all I had to do was figure out how to give the story a happy ending.

It seemed like I had just put my head on the pillow when it was time to get up! That was it, no more parties! It was fun and everything, but I was so tired that I felt nauseous. I had to leave the house for a little while, but I got back as quick as humanly possible. When I got back home there was one message on the answering machine ... Julian. He called to thank me for last night and to tell me again how good I looked. He laughed and asked me why I told Smokie that I was his secretary? He finished by saying that he knew I was tired because he was too, and that he'd call me back later, if I didn't call him first. I want that boy! There wasn't any way around it. I wanted to be with him.

I couldn't believe that I'd almost slept the entire day away. It was going on 5:00pm and I really hadn't accomplished a whole lot (besides getting some sleep). I guess I was a lot more tired then I thought. I never heard the phone ring, but I had three messages, one from Tracie (I forgot that I had told her and Kyme that I would hang out with them.). Oh, of course one of the messages was from Kyme, and the last one was a pleasant surprise, it was Julian again. I definitely couldn't hang out with him because I hadn't spent a weekend with my friends in weeks. They were going to start thinking that I was doing something that I didn't want them to know about. I called Tracie and Kyme back first and then I called Julian.

When I called Tracie there was no answer, so common sense told me that she was probably already at Kyme's place. I was right.

"Hi Kyme, where are we going and what are we doing today?"

First Kyme wanted to talk about where I had been all day. She's so nosey.

"So, you must have had a hot date because both Tracie and I tried to call you earlier and we both got your machine."

I told her that I did have a hot date and when she asked with whom I told her, "my bed." We both started laughing!

We decided to ride out to Landmark Park and walk around and do some people watching. There was some sort of festival going on, so if nothing else it would be interesting. I was nominated to drive because I wasn't in place when they called me the first time. I agreed to meet them at Kyme's apartment. As soon as I hung up the phone I called Julian.

"Hi Julian, I got your messages and you are most certainly welcome." I asked him what he was doing when I called and he said he was sitting there thinking about me.

So I said, "besides that?"

"I"m all partied out, so I thought I'd spend some time at home alone. Unless you want to come over?"

I gracefully declined his invitation because I "had" to spend some time with my friends. Julian and I wouldn't be doing anything besides sitting around the house alone anyway and I didn't know if that would be a really good thing to do. We made plans to see each other on Friday evening. We agreed that we'd decide what to do once we got together. We both hated to hang up the phone, but we did. It's not like Friday was "that" far away.

As I was driving over to Kyme's I wondered if now would be a good time to tell them about Julian? We had been seeing each other for almost four months and I thought it was about time that I started introducing him to my family and friends. I realized that it wasn't like I was going to end the relationship any time soon. I was way past the point of no return, way, way past it! When I finally arrived at Kyme's, she and Tracie immediately lit in on me for being so slow! This is a condition that I've suffered with since childhood. In my early twenties, I came to the conclusion that it was chronic. It does go into remission from time to time. If someone were to ask me if I was a punctual person I'd have to say, "No, but I am consistent (consistently late that is...)."

We piled into my car and headed for the park. Kyme wasn't going to be satisfied until she knew why I was so tired that day. I told them that I had gone out the night before and stayed out too late. So then I had to explain where I was the night before.

"Where were you last night," Tracie asked?

I told them that I had gone to a party out on the Point. They were surprised and wanted to know why I didn't take them with me? I didn't want to tell them about Julian while I was driving because I wanted to see the expressions on their faces. The next few minutes were filled with question after question; whose house was it; what did you wear; how did you get invited; who was there; what did the house look like; and finally the big question, who did you go with? Fortunately I saw a parking space and thought, "Okay, find a nice comfortable bench where we can sit and talk and then tell them about Julian." I didn't answer the last question.

"Y'all ask too many questions! Can I please park the car?"

They looked at each other then at me.

Kyme then said, "That's okay, you're gonna' tell us who you went to that party with before we leave this park today!"

Then they both started laughing!

Tracie looked at Kyme and said, "Shh, don't say any-thing else right now, she's trying to park the car!"

We all laughed as we walked toward the park.

The first vendor that we went to was an ice cream stand. We try not to eat a lot, but usually when we're together we just lose total control when it comes to food. As soon as we bought our ice cream I suggested we find a bench to sit down and eat.

I didn't know how to tell them about Julian, so I just started talking, "I met somebody!"

As soon as I said that Kyme asked, "Where, at the party?"

I responded, "No...the person I met invited me to the party. His name is Julian...Julian Brishard."

Before I could get another word out Tracie interrupted, "Isn't there a singer name Julian Brishard or Jules Brishard or something like that?"

I looked at both of them and said, "Yea, that's him. I met him at the Bistro after work one day."

They both started screaming, "Girl you went out with Jules Brishard? He is too fine!"

Tracie acted like she was falling down, "I can't believe you. You went out with him girl! I think I'm gonna' faint! What was it like?"

I smiled, "Let's see, he's a perfect gentleman, he's very nice and girl he smells good!"

I thought we were going to laugh so hard that we'd hyperventilate or break some ribs.

"So when are y'all going out again," Kyme asked?

I took a deep breath and told them that the party was actually not my first date with him, but that I had been seeing him for about four months. They both just looked at me.

Tracie asked, "Seeing him, for four months? You mean seeing him like dating him seeing him?"

I answered, "Uh, yea..."

"So why the big secret?   I thought we were your girls?" Kyme asked.

"Honestly, I don't think that either of you should be mad because you are my friends, my best friends! I didn't tell y'all about him at first because I really thought he and I would have a couple of dinners, a few laughs, and that would be it, but one day he told me he wanted more. With my divorce becoming final, you both know I wasn't ready to get involved with anyone. You know? Things with Julian started off fun, but now it's a little more then "just" fun. I'm still kind of overwhelmed by the whole thing. I thought about telling y'all a few times, but then I thought, "I'm dating Julian Brishard? This is crazy, what does he want with me?" After thinking about all of that foolishness I changed my mind about telling anybody. I'm telling y'all now because, well, you're my best friends and I want y'all to know."

Then I sat there quietly looking at them, waiting for

them to say something. For a minute they both just sat there looking back at me, sort of dumbfounded or like I was dumb, I couldn't tell.

Kyme was the first to say something. "Girl, you are too pitiful, just pathetic! Are you crazy? Nah, you're not crazy, you're just acting crazy!" It's not like we want to know every lurid detail of your little romance! Give me a break! I'm really hurt because we hadn't seen very much of you lately and we didn't know what was going on with you! Well, that's how I felt anyway.

Tracie never really had much to say.

"That pretty much sums it up for me too. I just didn't know what was happening with you. Even in the worst of times during your marriage we saw you just about every day, so for the last couple of months for you to withdraw from us was kind of weird for me because I didn't know what I could do to help you. I thought you were grieving over the divorce or something."

Kyme quickly interjected, "Oh, please..." (Kyme is not one who is ever at a loss for words.) "What would she have been grieving over? Losing someone who never loved her in the first place? Tracie, sometimes you just make me sick being so melodramatic! Let me shut up because I am really getting ready to let loose and say some things!"

Before I could open my mouth Tracie responded, "Yea...yea you're right, you do need to shut up before I have to jump down your throat for saying something you don't have any business saying!"

I don't often see Tracie upset, but when I do, it's usually over something Kyme has said or done! I politely interrupted what was the beginning of a fall out and reminded my dear friends that the subject at hand was my beau and not whether Tracie was a drama queen (because she is, but that's a whole 'nother story).

"Well, to make it up to you guys I'll just introduce y'all to Julian."

Before I could even say anything else Kyme blurted out, "When?"

Julian's such a busy man I didn't know when he'd be free, so I said I'd call him, but I already knew that they'd have to hold out until Friday. That was when Julian and I had planned to see each other anyway.

We spent the rest of our afternoon at the park laughing and talking about anything other then Julian. I don't know why I was so worried about telling them about him. Well, maybe it had something to do with thinking that I was in love with someone that I had only known for a few months. Before we went home, we stopped at Wing Wang's, our favorite Chinese restaurant, and had dinner. When I finally got home I didn't even bother sitting down, I went straight to the telephone and called Julian. There was no answer, so I left a message for him to call me when he got in.

CHAPTER

4

$\mathscr{I}$t was about 10:15pm and in his world that was still relatively early, but it was unusual for absolutely nobody to be there. I filled the bathtub with hot water, poured in a little bath oil, lit a couple of scented candles, and laid out my blue, silk nightie. By the time I got into the tub it was 10:45pm. It felt really good to sit there in the dark with my eyes closed. I needed to unwind from the day's activities. Being with Tracie and Kyme always wore me out and it was a big relief to finally tell them about Julian.

Just as I was about to doze off the telephone rang and of course it was Julian.

"Hey girl, I didn't wake you up did I? I got your message, so I'm returning your call. I feel like I haven't talked to you all day. The least that I could do is call to say good night."

"Hi Julian!"

He laughed.

"Hi Shelby."

We both laughed.

"Boy, you didn't even give me time to say hi or anything! What are you doing so full of energy at (and I looked at the clock) 11:15pm?" That's not really late for him, but he was talking like it was the middle of the afternoon.

"I did a lot of promotional stuff today, so I'm still a little wired. Once I sit down and relax I'll be all right. What were you doing when I called? Were you asleep?"

I didn't want to be a tease, but I answered anyway. "I'm unwinding by taking a candle lit bath."

For a couple of seconds there was silence, then with what I was sure was great restraint, Julian responded.

"Candle light bath, huh? Would it be forward of me to say I wish I was there?"

I thought, what the heck, tease him a little bit, "Now what would you be doing if you were here?"

He paused, I guess he was trying to place his words very carefully.

"I'd wait for you to finish your bath, then I'd give you a full body massage, and then I'd just hold you close to me all night long."

He's a liar! I'm sure he'd be trying to get in the tub with me or he'd be waiting for me to get out, so that he could try to have wild sex with me or something! I didn't say that to him though!

Instead I just said, "Oh, that sounds nice. Let me change the subject for a minute. I want you to meet my two best friends. Will you be home at all tomorrow evening?"

He laughed! I guess he was thinking that we were going to get all into the bath scene. I wasn't having it! If we had started talking about having sex, the next thing you know, we would have been doing it all over the place (having sex that is) and I really didn't want to do that.

Julian was glad that he was finally going to meet some of my friends. He told me that we could come over after 7:00pm the next evening. He said he was going to ask me to come by anyway. We stayed on the phone for about an hour. By that time I had gotten out of the tub, put on my nightie and was lying across the bed.

Before he hung up he asked, "You ready for that back rub yet?"

I smiled and said, "You sound a little tired. I'll take a rain check for another time when you're at full strength!"

He laughed and told me I was too much. We said good night, but not before he made me give him a good night kiss over the phone (he said it helped him to get to sleep every night). He's so silly...

The next morning I really didn't want to get up for work, so I lay in bed for a while, thinking about how well the day before had gone. I love my friends and I really want them to like Julian. I don't know why I spent so much energy worrying about the whole thing. As I drove to work, I hoped the kids had good weekends because I really wasn't ready to let go of "my" weekend yet. I had to do a lot of interacting with the students at the school where I worked as a Student Resource Specialist, which means I coordinate education and activities for students with behavioral and emotional problems. Put in laymen's terms, I'm a very high paid counselor. The kids that I work with are fourteen to eighteen years old and they're sent to me when they're too much trouble to keep in a traditional classroom setting, but not enough trouble to be kicked out of school or sent to jail. My job is very interesting and rewarding, and once I get the kids to trust me we become great friends. I have the cards, wedding invitations, birth announcements, and pictures to prove it. After the students graduate and go on with their lives' they never forget the ones who really cared enough to help them.

I was sure that the day would be just as eventful as every other day always proves to be. Kids drop by my office throughout the day to say hi or to talk about things going on in their lives. Most of the time I know that they just want someone to listen, but on the occasion when I'm asked for my opinion, I give it. I'm very straightforward and honest and I'm sure they know that or else they wouldn't keep coming back. I think it's also helpful that I'm not quite old enough to be considered a threat yet. I'm still cool.

CHAPTER
5

$\mathscr{I}$ could barely concentrate all morning because Kyme and Tracie were finally going to meet Julian. I thought we could meet at my place and then ride over to Julian's, to have dinner and then sit and talk. First I had to catch up with Julian, I wanted to remind him to let his cook, Miss Gladys, know that we were coming over for dinner. Miss Gladys cooks for Julian a few times a week and at special request (sort of like this last minute thing). She's about 68-70 years old, I imagine, and Julian just loves her to death. He has another woman, not quite as old as Miss Gladys that comes in three days a week to clean his house. He pays them all very well and he treats them like they're his grandmothers. He also has a driver that picks them up for work and then takes them home when they're finished. Now I ask you, how could I not love a man that is that thoughtful? I'm sure the way he treats them has a lot to do with him being raised by his mother, even though the only thing he has said to me about her is that she and I are really going to like each other. I've been told that she knows all about me.

Anyway, when I finally caught up with Julian I told him about dinner, about keeping it casual, and about it only being the four of us there, so that they could all get to know each other without any distractions. He agreed, said he'd just ask Miss Gladys to cook something good. Maybe some time in the future the girls could meet Smokie, but I didn't think it would be appropriate or comfortable, for all involved, if Smokie was there. He can really be a hand full at times. Julian agreed because he knew Smokie was out of control.

It seemed like the day was never going to end, but it did. Before going home I called Kyme and told her to pick Tracie up and meet me at my place at 6:30pm. Of course, there was a last minute crisis at work that had to be resolved and as if that wasn't enough, there was an accident on the way home that held traffic up for about twenty minutes. All of this extra stuff only took about 40 minutes or so, but it seemed like hours! By the time I drove into my parking lot I was really nervous. You would have thought that I was getting ready to take my mom and dad to meet Julian.

As I parked I thought, What if Kyme and Tracie don't like Julian?

What if Julian doesn't like them? When I was growing up I always had to deal with my friends not liking each other, but wanting to be my friends anyway, and you know what? It always worked itself out. Everybody simply tolerated each other for my sake (at least that's what I'd like to believe). In a small way this was a little different though.

As I walked into the house I glanced at the answering machine and I didn't have any messages. That was a good sign. I rushed into my bedroom and changed clothes. No sooner had I changed than the doorbell rang. I knew it was Kyme and Tracie, so I took my time and grabbed my purse as I headed for the door. There was really no reason for them to come in and get comfortable because for a change I was ready to go!

As I opened the door I greeted them, "Hi ladies!"

Both of them greeted me back, "Hey girl!"

And, as usual, Kyme had something to say. "I am absolutely shocked that you're ready!"

I smiled and looked at her and said, "Of course I'm ready. Why wouldn't I be?"

Tracie started laughing, "Girl, let's just go!"

As we drove to Julian's we sang, laughed, and talked. It seemed like we'd never get there, but we'd only been riding for fifteen minutes. As we got off of the interstate Tracie said she couldn't believe that she was actually going to get to see the inside of one of the houses in the neighborhood that we were in. I couldn't help but think, "Wait until she sees Julian's house..." The houses in his neighborhood are worth millions of dollars. Mostly professional athletes, entertainers, and CEO types live in the area.

As we approached his drive Kyme said, "Ooh, look at that one right there, a Mercedes convertible and a Range Rover. How much driving can one person do? Y'all know

I'm not into cars, but I would love to just sit in that Mercedes
with my shades on and the top down!"
Then she snapped her finger, threw her head back, and started laughing. I put on my turn signal and because Kyme was sitting in the front seat she almost broke my arm and my eardrum when she screamed and hit me.

"Ahh, I can't believe this! Is this his house?" Then she calmed down for a second and said, "You could have told us he was rolling in dough. We might be under dressed."

I couldn't think of a single thing to say except, "I just never thought about it..."

After we walked our way to the front door Tracie asked if she could ring the doorbell.

"Ooh girl, let me ring the doorbell. I never rang a doorbell at a house like this before."

I told her she was silly and she told me she knew that and to just move out of her way so she could ring the doorbell. When Julian opened the door he had on a pair of jeans, a white silk shirt (with the top two buttons undone), and a nice gold chain. He looked so good I wanted to push my friends out of the way and grab him by his collar and kiss him! But instead he welcomed us in and stepped aside. As I walked in he gently grabbed me by my waist and kissed me
on my right cheek. After kissing me he closed the door and extended his hand. As Tracie shook his hand he pulled her over and gave her a little hug and told her it was good to meet her. As usual, Kyme was in prime form, she laughing-

ly told Julian she didn't hug strangers. He laughed and said he didn't either, then he hugged her anyway.

Julian grabbed me by the hand and led us into the kitchen. I looked back at the girls as we were walking to the kitchen and they were being silly, mocking me and Julian as we held hands. I just smiled and told them to stop being bad. Julian stopped in the kitchen and told us we had to serve ourselves because Miss Gladys had gone home for the night.

Tracie then said, "Oh, you mean you don't have servants?"

Julian shook his head and said, "Actually I have an all male staff, but when I have beautiful women in my home I confine them to their quarters."

I just shook my head at both of them. We washed our hands in the bathroom between the kitchen and the dining room, fixed our plates, and headed for the dining room.

Miss Gladys out did herself as usual! She fixed Jamaican chicken, Italian stuffed squash, and steamed broccoli. For dessert we had key lime parfaits with chocolate cookie crumbs.

Kyme seemed to hit it off with Julian. "Julian, I thought your cook was an older black woman?"

His response was, "She is."

She then asked, "Well then, where are the collard greens, the rice, and the pig feet?"

We all laughed!

We had a great time during dinner. When we finished

Julian offered to clean off the table and serve dessert. Kyme and Tracie protested and insisted on doing it themselves, but Julian won out. He asked me to help him carry the dishes to the kitchen. As we were rinsing the dishes off and putting them in the dishwasher Julian stood behind me and kissed me on the back of my neck.

"Come on boy, we have people in the other room waiting for dessert."

When I turned around to face him he said, "I know, but I'm trying to get my dessert, here in the kitchen, right now."

When he kissed me all I could think about was how weak I was getting. Julian was wearing me down in more ways then one. Because of his weight I lost my footing and fell up against the open dishwasher door and knocked some of the dishes around in the rack. Kyme hollered from the other room.

"Y'all okay in there? Do you need some help?"

Julian hollered back, "No, we have everything under control, we're trying to get dessert!"

He looked at me and kind of squinted his eyes, smiled, and gave me another peck on the lips.

We had dessert in Julian's entertainment room and laughed and talked until 10:00 pm. I was glad that my best friends were getting a long with my "new" friend. At one point during the conversation I actually had to get up and leave the room. I stepped out on the patio and walked toward the pool and looked at the reflection of the moon in the water. I closed my eyes for just a second and took in the coolness of the breeze that was blowing. My contentment was overwhelming. I shook my head, smiled to myself, and turned around and went back into the house. As I approached the entertainment room I could hear Kyme talking. The tone of the conversation sounded a little more serious then it did before I left, so I slowed my pace to listen to what was being said. I could vaguely make out bits and pieces. It sounded like Kyme was telling Julian that they loved me very much...that I had been through a whole lot in the last few years...that I deserved to be happy....she could tell that I cared a lot for him...didn't want to see me hurt again...was he going to ask me to marry him? At this point I kind of lowered my head and put my hand up to my mouth. While I was waiting to hear Julian's response, Tracie walked up behind me and almost scared me to death.

"Whatcha' doing Shelby?"

I didn't scream, but that was only because my hand was covering my mouth. I turned around and looked at Tracie and hit her on the arm.

"You scared me!"

She started laughing and said, "If you hadn't been creeping, you wouldn't have been scared!"

I never heard the end of the conversation because when Tracie and I walked into the room Kyme and Julian stopped talking and looked at us. Julian grabbed me by my hand, pulled me over to him, and kissed me on the cheek.

I looked at him and asked, "What was that for?"

He looked at me and said, "Because I...I wanted to. I

thought it was okay for me to do that."

I looked at him and thought, "Boy, if you only knew!"

At this point I thought it was a good time to ask the ladies if they were ready to go because we all had to go to work the next morning. Julian walked us out to the car. He and I held hands as we walked. When we got to the car Kyme gave him a really (really) big hug and a kiss on the cheek. Tracie hugged him too, but instead of her kissing him, he kissed her on the cheek. While they were getting in the car Julian walked around to the driver's side, gently cupped my face with both of his hands, and kissed me on the forehead. As he was opening the car door he thanked "me" for a great evening. After I got into the car Julian stuck his head in the car window to talk with Tracie and Kyme.

"Now that y'all know where I live, you don't have to be strangers!"

They both said okay and we were on our way. As I was pulling away Julian told me to call him when I got home.

During the ride home Kyme and Tracie couldn't say enough nice things about Julian.

At one point I even said, "This is just your first time meeting him and y'all know all of that from just one evening?"

It's kind of ironic, but after my first evening at the restaurant with Julian I thought I knew him too! When I got home I gave both of my friends their hugs in the parking lot and we agreed to talk the next evening. I went into my condo and headed straight for my bedroom. I got ready for bed and then I called Julian. His phone only rang once before he picked it up.

"We made it home safely Julian, you can go to bed now."

He laughed softly and said, "Thanks for calling. I enjoyed your friends tonight. They both seem like really nice ladies. I meant what I said, they're welcome here any time."

Before we hung up I tried to get him to tell me what he and the girls had talked about, especially Kyme, but he wouldn't tell me. I didn't press him about it.

CHAPTER

6

At this point in our relationship I knew I wanted to be more than Julian's friend, much more. How could I not? He seemed to have every quality that I had always looked for in a man. He was strong, but not real hard and when he was dealing with women it was like a man handling a baby. He was gentle and attentive, but not demeaning or disrespectful. I loved the way he looked at me when I talked. He made me feel like the only thing that mattered for that very moment was what I was saying. He also made me feel beautiful, sexy, sophisticated, and sensuous. After three years of being mistreated, verbally and mentally abused, made to feel like I was ugly, stupid, and ignorant, yes...Julian was just the breath of fresh air that I needed. If he wasn't what I needed, he was sure what I wanted! In the four months that I had been with him I hadn't even thought about my ex-husband. I decided that I was going to do this and as the saying goes, "It was all good!" After having dinner with Julian and "the girls." He called me at work the following morning to tell me that some promotional opportunities had come available and he had to leave town in an hour and a half. He would be gone for about two weeks. I was very disappointed, but I understood, this was the nature of the business he was in. He told me that he would call me as soon as he could, but he wouldn't be calling late and waking me up. We did our little "kissy, kissy" over the phone and then we hung up. I really didn't care how late it was, as long has he called. As soon as I hung up I started missing him.

I was really surprised when, three days later, Friday evening rolled around and I hadn't heard from Julian. I was getting kind of worried. Around 8:30pm my phone rang and my heart stopped because I knew it was Julian. I was going to be upset if it was anybody else. When I answered the phone I tried not to sound too excited.

"Hello..." The voice on the other end was not Julian's, but it did sound familiar.

"Hey baby! What'cha doin?"

I thought, "How did this fool get my number?" So I quickly responded because I didn't have time for games. "Who is this? I would advise you to answer quickly because I'm getting ready to hang up."

When I heard the deep, throaty laugh I knew who it was so I said, "Smokie..."

He laughed some more and finally said, "If it makes you feel better you can call me Julian, with your sexy self!"

I didn't know why Smokie had my number, but common sense told me that he had gotten it from Julian.

"Did Julian tell you to call me?"

Smokie is definitely one of those kind of guys that won't take no for an answer. No matter what you say to him, you can't hurt his feelings or insult him because his ego is too big.

"Shelby, Shelby, Shelby, can't I just call to check on you? Julian is out of town and I know you have to be a little lonely. Do you want to go out for dinner tonight?"

I could just imagine Smokie grinning from ear to ear.

"Smokie, is Julian okay, did he tell you to call me? Better yet, give me his number and I'll call him, okay?"

Smokie was not quite finished yet.

"Look, Julian asked me to call and check on you and I'm doing that. I take my responsibilities to my "boy" very seriously. Now, can I come over there and take care of you? In the past Julian and I have shared everything. I don't see why it should stop now."

I would have been amused, but I didn't know if Smokie was serious or joking. Instead I became annoyed with his conversation.

"Look, I don't have time to play games with you Smokie! If Julian asked you to check on me then fine, you've done it. If he didn't then I would advise you to lose my number and not call me again! I'll pretend like we never had this conversation and when you do talk to Julian, you have 'him' call me! Good night Smokie."

Of course, instead of getting mad Smokie laughed.

"I knew you weren't as quiet as you looked! I love a woman who speaks her mind. You have a good night and sleep tight. I'll talk to you later."

He continued to laugh as he hung up. Smokie is a trip!

Julian finally called two days later. He apologized profusely and had flowers sent to me. His schedule had been more rigorous then he had expected, so he wasn't able to call me like he wanted to. He was leaving the hotel too early in the morning and getting back too late at night. He was unusually thoughtful like that. When we talked I found that I wasn't mad at all, I missed him too much. I felt the sting of reality slapping me in my face though. I would probably have quite a few sleepless nights.

One of my sisters and two of my brothers were coming to visit. We always had a great time when we got together. This time things would be even better because I was going to introduce them to Julian. I was so excited about them meeting him that I didn't know what to do with myself. My plan was to have Julian over for dinner their first night in town and afterwards we could hang out at my house or we could go somewhere for drinks. Their second night in town would be big fun because I had asked Julian if he would invite a few of his celebrity friends over for a casual little get together. I figured two days of planned activities was enough. The rest of their visit could be played by ear.

Since my family would be flying in on a Thursday afternoon I thought I'd work half a day. I'd gone to the grocery store the night before and gotten everything except the seafood that we were going to have for dinner. I thought maybe we'd have crab legs, shrimp, oysters, clams, grouper fingers, hush puppies, and salad. I always had lemonade in my refrigerator, a couple of bottles of white zinfandel and a case of sodas in the cabinet, so drinks were covered.

CHAPTER

7

*F*ortunately my day was pretty uneventful. One of my favorite students came by my office to shoot the breeze right before it was time for me to leave. Of course, my very first thought was a selfish one, "I hope Sergio isn't having a crisis today because I'm leaving in 30 minutes!" But I didn't say that.

"Hi Mr. Stanton! What can I do for you today?" Sergio is one of the more colorful students at the school. He's very intelligent, very creative, and very talented. Did I mention that he was also very "witty" and had a great sense of humor? If I were in high school he would definitely be the kind of boy that I'd be chasing behind. It's because of his fantastic personality that I've had to talk with him and his girlfriend, as well as six other female students (10th through 12th grade). All of who were willing to do anything short of killing each other to be with him. Oh yeah, and one student teacher came to talk with me once because she was afraid that she was going to lose her job because she enjoyed flirting with him.

Anyway, Sergio had a seat and told me what was on

his mind. "Hi Miss Simone. I haven't been by to talk with you in a while. I wanted to see how you were doing."

I was flattered that he was thinking about my welfare.

"Well, isn't that nice of you Sergio. I'm doing just fine. You know you guys keep me on my toes. Speaking of which, how are you and your girlfriend doing these days?"

Sergio, always quick to respond, "You talking about Mia? We broke up. We decided that we should be friends. You know she's leaving for Howard University as soon as she graduates. I ain't tryin' to get played! I know how the program works. Mia will leave here all in love, meet her a knuckle head up the way, and then she'll send me a letter talkin' bout we can be friends. I think we can skip all that foolishness and be friends right now! Don't you agree Miss Simone?"

I personally thought that was a very mature decision.

"Well Sergio, I feel like you're thinking very realistically. When people go off to college they do make a lot of new friends and they definitely establish new relationships. How did Mia feel about your decision?"

"She didn't like it! She tried to tell me why we should stay together and then she started cryin'. What's up with girls cryin' all the time Miss Simone?"

Men and boys are just alike when it comes to women crying. They don't have a clue. I finally answered him.

"Well, maybe she cares about you Sergio, you ever thought about that?"

I knew Sergio wouldn't disappoint me with some weak

excuse.

"Of course I thought about it! I care about her too Miss Simone. It ain't like that! I just think it's better to take care of business right now. We'll both be all right. She's going off to college and I got another year in high school. I'm a lot of things, but I ain't stupid!"

I smiled at Sergio and agreed with him, he wasn't stupid.

"I agree, you're not stupid and you've made a very mature decision. You're right, both of you will be all right. I just have one question. Why did you break up now, there're still four months left in the school year?"

Sergio grinned at me and said, "Well, I just wanted to be able to mend my broken heart while I still had girls around to help me heal."

I looked at Sergio and asked him to go to lunch because I realized that even though he made a seemingly mature decision, he had only made it because he wanted to play the field.

"I hate to end this wonderful conversation, but I have to leave and you really should go and get yourself something to eat. As usual though, I've thoroughly enjoyed talking with you."

Sergio left my office to finish his lunch. After he left I closed up shop and left for the airport.

I excitedly walked out to my car. I hadn't seen my family in months and I knew we were going to have a great time. Kary, my oldest sister, was married and had two kids, so she couldn't come and Kristoff, my oldest bother, who was also married couldn't come either. My twin brother and sister, Collin and Sharrin, and my youngest bother Coleman were coming. I knew they were going to be surprised by how great a time they were going to have! I went to pick up the seafood and then I headed for the airport. When I arrived at the airport their flight had just landed, so I parked my car and walked to the baggage claim area to meet them.

Sharrin is kind of bossy, so I was sure she'd be leading the way to the baggage claim area. When I finally saw them, sure enough, Sharrin was walking ahead of the guys. Collin and Coleman were lagging behind checking out women. Both Collin and Sharrin are in serious relationships, but I think Collin's girlfriend is more serious about the relationship then he is (I think that's a female thing). Coleman on the other hand is "dating" several people. If you ask him about it he'll say that he has a lot of friends that he hangs out with. We did a group hug, before they checked me out to see if I had gained any weight or if I had cut my hair. Being the youngest girl, my family is always assessing my appearance. I know that it's done out of love. Both my mom and dad were athletic in their hey day. The also did a little modeling. So, my siblings think we should look like movie stars at all times.

They had eaten a little snack on the airplane so I didn't think it was necessary to stop for lunch. I had plenty of things at my house for them to munch on if they got hungry. I was excited at the idea that Julian was going to final-

ly meet my family. It was going to be interesting to see the
looks on their faces when they found out that I'd been dating a celebrity. I hadn't told them that anybody was coming
over for dinner because I wanted it to be a surprise. I knew
Coleman was going to be especially pleased because he's into
rubbing elbows with the "beautiful people." I thought he'd
probably harass Julian about women all night. I have to
admit, Coleman is spoiled rotten and it's no thanks to the
whole family. He's not a gigolo or anything, but he is a little too carefree about life.

We spent the better part of the afternoon talking about
my parents and my other brother and sister. I laugh hardest
when I'm around my family because we crack on each other
like it's going out of style. If my Mom and Dad had come
we really would have been laughing because they are truly
characters. Collin and Kristoff have the best sense of humor
out of all of us. They can tell a story like nobody's business;
sound effects, facial expressions, the whole nine yards.
Around 4:30pm I decided I needed to take a nap because I
knew it was going to be a long night. Everybody else was
crashing anyway, that is, everybody except Coleman. Coco
(as we call him) wanted to go riding. I wouldn't give him
my keys so he settled for watching TV, but he wanted me to
promise him that I wouldn't keep him confined to my house
all weekend.

It was 6:00pm before I knew it, so I got up and started
getting dinner ready. Coco never went to sleep or else he
only slept for a minutes because he came in the kitchen to

help me.   I swear that boy only thinks about one thing...women.

"So Shell, do you have any single friends that I can hang out with while I'm here? They can be single, divorced, or separated, it doesn't matter, as long as nobody comes looking for her while we're out."

I looked at my brother and shook my head no. I told him that I had no single friends that he would be interested in or that would be interested in him. In addition to everything else, Coco also has the biggest ego in the whole family. He is of the opinion that every woman he meets will fall in love with him sooner or later. What's scary is that a lot of them do!

When the doorbell rang I shouted that I'd get the door. I wanted Julian to have a grand entrance.

Sharrin, in her special way asked, "Who's coming over right at dinner time?"

When I opened the door I gave Julian a kiss, grabbed his hand, and escorted him into the living room. When we entered the room I announced that I had someone special that I wanted them to meet.

"Sharrin, come here! I have someone here that I want all of you to meet!"

When she walked into the room her mouth literally fell open, "Don't we know him from somewhere?"

I smiled and said, "Julian, this is my sister Sharrin, my brothers Coleman and Collin. Guys this is my 'little honey' Julian Brishard."

Sharrin, being the most vocal of the three, maintained her composure, but reprimanded me for keeping such a secret.

"Shell, it's just like you not to tell anyone in the family that you were dating someone. Girl, you know this is the kind of stuff you should tell your sisters!"

Then she addressed the rest of her comment to Julian.

"You have to excuse us because our little sister not only didn't tell us that someone was coming to dinner, she didn't tell us that she had been seeing anybody ... and look who walks through the door 'YOU' Julian Brishard! It's really a pleasure to meet you, it really is!"

Collin got up to shake Julian's hand and simply said, "Nice to meet you man! How'd you have time to meet my sister with all of those fine women in your videos? You gonna' have to hook a brother up?"

Julian laughed and said, "Your sister ain't so bad. It's good to finally meet some of Shelby's family. She didn't tell me that I was going to be a surprise guest. I thought y'all knew that I was coming by."

We got past all of the 'hello's' and had dinner. It was great! Of course, it's pretty hard to mess up seafood when all you're doing is steaming, frying, and broiling. After dinner we sat down, had a few drinks, and talked.

During the course of the conversation Coco asked Julian when he would introduce him to some of the ladies in his videos.

"Look man, we're leaving Sunday night, so I have to

move fast. You know I don't mean to sweat a brother, but I don't have much time to waste."

Julian looked at him and said, "Do you need to meet them before tomorrow? Then he looked over at me, "Oh, I guess since Shelby didn't tell y'all that I was coming by for dinner, she also didn't tell y'all that you'd be hanging out at my house tomorrow night?"

Sharrin looked at me and said, "Can we please agree that there will be no more surprises Shell?"

I laughed and said, "Okay, no more surprises, I promise! I can't even be nice to you people!"

That was all Coco needed to hear. The party was going to be at Julian's. Julian suggested that we bring a change of clothes because he seemed to think that we wouldn't want to drive back to my place after partying all night. I figured it would be safe to stay, it's not like Julian and I would be there alone. There would be a house full of people, in addition to my sister and both of my brothers. Cool! We were going to spend the night at Julian's house.

Friday morning we hung around my place watching talk shows. By mid-afternoon we were dressed, so we decided to go out to lunch and to do a little shopping. I told everybody that the party would be casual and that it wasn't necessary to go out and spend crazy money to look good. Personally, I already knew what I was going to wear. I just had to buy it. A week or so before I had seen a black midi skirt with a long sleeved, black mock turtleneck, and some black ankle boots and I had the perfect black leather belt to where with it. I knew where I needed to go, so after eating lunch Sharrin and I headed one way and the guys another. We agreed to meet back in front of the restaurant in three hours. It didn't take Sharrin long to find an outfit. She settled on a leopard print top and a little brown spandex mini skirt. I had to admit it was rather cute, but a little "too" short and "too" snug for my taste. When Sharrin tried on her outfit she came out of the dressing room for me to see her in it.

"What do you think Shell? Be honest because I want to look good tonight!"

I looked at her with my head tilted and said, "Now you know what I think! I think it's too short, but since I know that's not what you want to hear...it looks good."

Sharrin was satisfied, actually I know my sister, so I knew she had already decided to get the outfit before she came out of the dressing room, she just wanted to hear somebody else say she looked good in it.

We went and bought shoes and then we met up with the guys. Coco had gotten a pair of black jeans and a yellow mock polo turtleneck with a black stripe around the top of the neck. He was going to wear it with his black Lugz boots. Collin bought a purple DKNY shirt to wear with a pair of black slacks and a pair of black, double buckle Kenneth Cole boots. After we reviewed each other's purchases we headed home. Once we arrived at my house we talked and packed. By the time we finished it was 6:00pm or so. We piled into my car and drove on over to Julian's place to get ready for the party.

CHAPTER
8

When Coco saw Julian's house I thought he was going to lose his mind! He went into this whole dialogue about being in his "element."

"I like what I see and this is where I'm supposed to be! This is my element. I've been trying to tell y'all this for years."

We went through the gate to the back of the house where the limo was parked. I could see the Range Rover parked in the garage, so Julian must have driven his Mercedes. We walked in through the kitchen and I introduced everybody to Miss Gladys, who was on her way home. Mr. Vestas was waiting for her in his apartment over the garage. He was going to take her home and then come back to his apartment. Julian had asked Miss Gladys to tell us to relax and make ourselves at home. The hors d'oeurves were set up and the only thing that needed to be done was to uncover the platters when we were ready to start the party. Miss Gladys explained that a couple of servers would be showing up later to work the party and replenish the food as necessary.

Sharrin and I went upstairs and picked a room at the opposite end of the hall from Julian's room. It was the only bedroom that had two full beds. Coco and Collin got separate rooms closer to Julian's. I could only imagine what Coco's plans were. Once we settled in and unpacked I took everyone on a quick tour of the house. Since we were upstairs we started with Julian's bedroom. Coco was surprised to see that one entire wall of the room was mirrored.

"Brother-man is a little too conservative to have mirrors all over the place, isn't he?"

I started laughing and said, "Coco, some people just appreciate the decorative quality of mirrors, thank you very much!"

We all laughed! Coco said he would ask Julian about the mirrors because they added a nice touch to the master bedroom. I had no additional comments.

After touring the entire house we sat in the entertainment room. Collin had been pretty quiet, so I was really surprised when he asked to hear some of Julian's music.

"Obviously Julian can blow, all we have to do is look at the size of his house and listen to the radio to know that he can make money. Does he have anything around that's not electronically enhanced?"

I was insulted because I thought Collin was insinuating that Julian was one of the "electronically enhanced" performers that we so often hear on the radio (who couldn't perform live at a concert no matter how much money you paid them). I had never heard his vocals on tape and had honestly never thought about asking, but inspite of that I came to Julian's defense.

"Collin, come on! You don't really think that Julian can't sing? You said yourself he can blow, you hear him on the radio all the time! I've never heard his vocals on tape, but he has sung to me on occasion, so let me assure you that his voice is not electronically enhanced in any way."

Sharrin stood up and walked across the room towards Julians' CD collection.

"I don't care if the brother couldn't sing a note. He could just stand in the room and never open his mouth as far as I'm concerned. Collin have you ever looked at him? The man is "faune!" If he can't sing, shame on him!" Realizing that I had taken offense to what he said, Collin tried to clear up the misunderstanding.

"Look, I know he can sing! I just wanted to hear his vocals, a little acapella is all I'm asking for, a song without instruments, or electronics!"

I calmed down a bit and said, "Oh, then that's what you should have said. I thought you were implying that Julian couldn't sing. The answer to your question is, I don't know."

Coco looked at me and said, "Girl, you losing it! You 'bout to catch up with Sharrin."

We all looked at each other and laughed.

When Julian finally arrived it was about 8:45pm. We were still sitting in the entertainment room listening to music and to Coco talk trash about who he was going to meet that night at the party. We also had to hear what he was going to tell his boys when he got back home. He knew they were going to be jealous when they heard about the good time he had.

Coco hugged me. "Thank you for being my best sister and for making this trip the bomb!"

I pushed him away and said, "Coco, I'm insulted! I can't believe that your coming to see me this weekend wouldn't have been the bomb even if we weren't hanging out with Julian. I don't know what to think about that statement."

He laughed and said, "You know what I mean, this is more then any of us expected. This is going to be mad fun you know, hanging out with celebrities and everything."

Then he insulted me again by saying, "Who would have thought that our little sister would ever date a celebrity and one so large?"

I looked at him and told him that if he didn't stop while he was ahead I was going to have to smack him.

I could hear Julian shouting through the house, "Shelby and family where are you? Make some noise so I can find you."

I left the room to go greet Julian. When I found him he was coming down the hall. I stopped him and gave him a kiss.

He put his arms around me and said, "I could get used to this, you know! Give me one more."

We kissed again and by this time Coco came looking

for us. "Okay, there's plenty of time for that. We're only in town for the weekend, so please, let's try not to be rude to the guests."

He and Julian shook hands and we walked back to find Collin and Sharrin.

When we got back to the entertainment room Coco wanted to know who was coming to the party. Julian said he really wasn't sure and went on to explain that the word just had to go out that there was going to be a party and folks would show up, people in the business and the full time groupies. He went on, "Man, there are people that party every night of the week. People still get off on house parties, so I can guarantee that this place will be packed by 1:00am."

I looked at him and said, "1:00a.m, I was hoping things would be wrapped up by then?"

Julian looked at me and said, "Baby, a truly "good" party doesn't really get started until about 1:00am, but because y'all are guest in my home I'm starting at 11:00pm and locking the doors at about 3:00am or 4:00am. Your family wanted a party, so I'm trying to give them a party!"

I looked at him and said, "Are the food and drinks going to last that long?"

Julian told me that there was no way that folks would stay at a house party if it ran out of food or drinks, so not to worry about it because Miss Gladys knows the deal. He was sure if we checked the pantry we would find more liquor and if we checked the refrigerator in the pantry we would find more food. The bartender would be at the house by 10:00pm to check the stock, so there was nothing for us to do except relax and enjoy the party. I already knew that I was going to bed at about 1:00am. I had no desire to stay up partying after 2:00am.

As he did a little dance Coco sang, "Oh yea! I'm ready to get my dance on right now!"

At 12:30pm the party was going strong. As I walked around I saw a few faces that I recognized, Puff Daddy, one of the guys from Boyz to Men, and Erykah Badu. I even recognized some of the dancers from videos that I had seen on BET. I thought I saw Maia Campbell, the young girl from "In The House" (LL Cool J's show). If I didn't know any better I would say I saw Tyra Banks and a couple of other models. People were everywhere dancing, drinking, eating, hanging out by the pool, just everywhere I looked. I danced a few times with Julian and told him not to worry about me, to entertain his guest, I'd mingle. One person I hadn't seen all night was Smokie. In a strange way I sort of missed his presence because with his "special" personality he could definitely liven up a party.

I saw Sharrin dancing and she looked like she was having a good time. As I looked at her I thought, "She looks really good tonight. I know a lot of the men have been checking her out."

I hadn't seen Collin in a while, but Coco was all over some chick trying to get his "rap on." She was probably a groupie because she didn't look like any entertainer that I recognized. I was shocked when I glanced around at the staircase and saw Collin coming from upstairs with some drop-dead gorgeous woman.

I looked at him and just shook my head, and because he was walking behind her, he shrugged his shoulders and mouthed, "What can I say?"

As I was looking at him Julian walked up behind me and hugged me around my waist. "What are you doing?"

I turned around to face him, "Nothing, just looking at all of the pretty people."

He hugged me and asked, "Is everything all right?"

I shook my head and said, "Of course, but I'm getting tired because it's way past my bed time. I think I might call it a night in a little while."

He hugged me a little tighter and said, "Shelby you can't go to bed now, the party is just getting started!"

I just looked up at him and without saying a word he understood what I was thinking.

"Okay, I know, you're not a party person. Just let me know when you get ready to go upstairs. I want to talk with you before you go to sleep."

I said, "Okay, I'll find you. I just want to let Sharrin know that the bedroom door will be locked, so she'll have to knock to get in. I'll find you in a few minutes."

I couldn't imagine what Julian would want to talk about at this time of night and I was too tired to try to figure it out. When I found Sharrin, she was talking with some guy, so she introduced me.

"This is my sister Shelby..."

Before she could get another word out of her mouth he looked directly in my eyes and said, "I see beauty definitely runs in your family."

He extended his hand and introduced himself, "I'm Ginuwine. It's a pleasure to meet you."

I said, "Oh, it's nice meeting you too! I like your 'I'll Do Anything.' It's really nice."

Then I looked at Sharrin and told her that I was going to bed and for her to knock when she was ready to get into the room. I shook Ginuwine's hand again and left to look for Julian.

As I was looking for Julian I passed a woman that looked vaguely familiar. She was huddled with three other women talking. Suddenly it dawned on me where I had seen her before. She was the one that stared me up and down when I went to that party on the Point with Julian. She was an ex-girlfriend of Julian's. She posed no threat to me though ... I had him now. When I found Julian he was out by the pool being a gracious host. I excused myself and told him that I was on my way to bed. He grabbed my hand and whispered go on up, I'll be there in a minute. The music wasn't too loud so I knew I would fall asleep as soon as my head hit the pillow and I could hardly wait.

There was a TV in my bedroom, so I turned it on. Instead of changing my clothes I just stretched out across the bed. I thought I'd wait until Julian left to get undressed. I didn't want to start anything I couldn't finish. I heard a knock at the door and I figured it had to be Julian because Sharrin was too into Ginuwine to be coming up to bed now.

I sat up and said, "Come in ..."

Julian opened the door with two glasses of wine, and a piece of paper in his hands.

I looked at him and said, "Where are you going with all of that wine?"

He smiled and said, "I brought you a night cap and I thought it rude to let you drink alone."

He smiled as I reached for the glass. I couldn't resist asking, "You wouldn't be trying to get me drunk to take advantage of me, would you?"

He laughed out loud and responded, "I hope I wouldn't have to get you drunk to take advantage of you."

All I could say was "Oh!"

I took a sip of wine from my glass and Julian started talking. He handed me the piece of paper he was holding and told me it was his first concert schedule. I looked it over from top to bottom. He was going to be gone for the months of February and March. His tour started in Atlanta and finished in Phoenix. In between, he would go to Baltimore, New York, Hartford, Worchester, Pittsburgh, Hampton, Greensboro, Orlando, Miami, Oklahoma City, Denver, Houston, St. Louis, Dallas, Seattle, Sacramento, San Jose, and Los Angeles. We had never been apart for that long, so I got kind of quiet. He must have sensed my apprehension because he started comforting me.

"Don't get emotional on me. I didn't show the schedule to you for you to get sad."

I looked at him, while holding up the schedule, and said, "This is a long time to be away from each other. It's going to be kind of hard."

He took a sip of his wine and shook his head, "I know, I was thinking the same thing. That's why I want you to come to my first concert and then to any other concerts that you want to come to. Of course, I'll be paying for everything."

I must have looked at him dumbfounded because he said, "Close your mouth! I want you to do what you want to do, but I really want you at my first concert and then I was thinking that maybe you could come to one more in February and then two in March. That way we'll get to see each other every other week or at least four times while I'm on the road. What do you think?"

I hugged him and said, "That's a good idea! I'd like that!" I sat back and looked at him with tears in my eyes and said, "You know you spoil me, right?"

I bit on my bottom lip as he said, "No, I don't spoil you. I love you."

Nobody could tell me that hearing him say he loved me didn't deserve a kiss. I knew that I loved him, but I was still a little gun shy from my marriage, not quite ready to say those three words yet, and even though it felt like we'd been together forever, it had only been six months.

I don't remember sitting my glass down on the nightstand, but I guess I must have. Julian was on top of me kissing me. I could feel his hand going under my shirt. My brain was saying, "Whoa, slow this down! Slow your roll girlfriend, slow your roll!" But my mouth was not cooperating and my body was like, "Okay, this feels good, this feels right!"

Julian whispered in my ear, "Baby, I love you so much. I would go crazy without you for two whole months."

All I could manage to say was, "I would miss you too."

He was rubbing my stomach with one hand and holding the back of my head with the other.

Then he asked, "Can I make love to you Shelby?"

I was going to say yes, I really was, but then the door flew open! Julian sat up, looked at the intruder and said, "The party is downstairs man." I heard a response, "Oops, sorry, my bad!" and then the door closed.

We sat up and looked at each other awkwardly until I said, "I'm tired, I think I'm going to go to bed now."

Julian slowly stood up, "Okay, I guess I should go back downstairs. I am having a party, huh?" He gave me a peck on the lips and said good night! As he left the room he turned around and said, "Make sure you lock the door."

The weeks went by quickly. Julian wanted me at his first concert, so I made sure that I was there to cheer him on. I almost became jealous listening to the women in the audience scream his name. They were totally out of control! Fortunately Julian arranged for me to have a bodyguard. I felt relatively safe in the event that someone in the audience figured out that I was his lady. His concert lasted for 2 1/2 hours. At the end of his performance I walked up and gave him two dozen roses. It's amazing how thousands of rolling eyes feel when they're staring at you at the same time. For a moment it felt very special to be the envy of every woman in the theater, even if they didn't know that "I" was really the one that he was singing to. I was glad that I made it to the first concert because it was a hit. All of the reviews talked about how smooth and sultry he was. How sexy he danced and how he had every woman in the theater in the palm of his hand.

Back stage was crowded. I had to literally fight my way through the crowd. Well, my bodyguard had to fight my way through the crowd. It was so crowded that I almost thought I wasn't going to be able to see him until he got back to the hotel. When I first arrived in Atlanta I went straight to the hotel and even though I knew Julian was there somewhere I didn't try to see him. I didn't want to distract him. When I finally made my way to his dressing room Julian was in the process of asking someone if they had seen me. As soon as he turned around and saw me he walked over and gave me a sweet, sweaty kiss. He was soaking wet. I had never seen a singer up-close after a performance, so I didn't realize how much energy they used on the stage.

He smiled and said, "Thank you for coming! When did you get here, to Atlanta I mean?"

I told him that I had been there since 3:00pm that afternoon.

He looked at me kind of surprised and asked, "Why didn't you come by my room or call me?"

I explained that I thought he didn't need to see me before he performed. I was reprimanded on the spot and told not to ever do that again. In the future he wanted me to check in, get myself situated, and at the very least call him to let him know that I was there. I assured him that I would do just that from now on.

We rode back to the hotel together. One body guard road in the car with us and two others rode in another limo behind us. When we pulled up to the Hotel Nikko groupies were already all over the place, so we went around to a back entrance that would allow us an escape to an underground garage. As we were getting out of the car Julian looked over at me and asked, "Baby, you are coming to the after party right?"

I shook my head, "No, that was not part of our agreement! I said I would come to your concerts, but I have no intention of going to any of the after parties. You go on to the party and we can meet for lunch or brunch tomorrow. You know I'm not into all of that partying!"

Julian did a sad face and said, "Not even for a little while?"

I looked at him and said, "Not even for a little while. I don't even want to see the room where the party is. You go on and enjoy yourself. I can see you in the morning."

Julian held my hand and as we walked in he told me that he wouldn't be at the party long, just long enough to make an appearance. I wasn't concerned because my plan was to go to my room, take a shower, watch a little TV, and then go to sleep.

The next morning Julian and I worked out, had breakfast in his suite, and spent the morning talking. For lunch we went to Planet Hollywood, just to get out of the hotel. I hung out with him later in the afternoon when he went to the theater to sound test his equipment. I decided that I would wait for him at the hotel and skip his Saturday night performance. Sunday morning we worked out in the hotel spa and later had breakfast. The rest of the day we hung out in the hotel and watched videos. I flew home after Julian's Sunday performance. One concert down and three to go...

While Julian was on the road I hung out with Tracie and Kyme. Sometimes we rented videos and went to Julian's house to watch them on the movie screen in his entertainment room. We used his weight room to workout and we even spent the night at his house a couple of nights. This was my way of making up for not inviting them to the party that Julian had for my family in January. I sincerely forgot about them. As the self appointed keeper of all of the important people in my life, that would have been too many people for me to try to keep up with at one time.

After every concert I came back and gave Tracie and Kyme a blow by blow of where I stayed and what I did while I was there, how the women acted during and after the concert, and anything else news worthy. My girlfriends knew that I would neglect them when Julian got back to town, but they weren't mad, they understood. Once while we were together, Kyme asked me if I had told Julian that I loved him yet.

I looked at her and said, "Please, why would I tell him that?"

She shook her head and said, "You ought to be ashamed of yourself for acting like that. You know we know, right? You can try and fool yourself, but that's the only person that you're fooling!"

Tracie even knew that I loved him. "Shelby, you talk with him almost every night. You've traveled to four different cities to be with him, just so y'all wouldn't miss each other so much during the two months he's on the road. You have keys to his house and you know the code to the alarm. Girl, you look at that man like you're just going to eat him up. Both of you are just oblivious to anything and anybody else that might have the misfortune of being in a room with you. Now, I'm thinking, somebody loves somebody in this whole thing. Everybody knows that Julian loves you, so I'm just guessing when I say you love him too! You know I'm usually the last one to find out these things, but y'all aren't the least bit difficult to figure out."

I had to admit it. I did love him, but I wasn't going to tell him that, or anybody else for that matter. We hadn't been together long enough for me to expose myself to him like that. I had to know for myself that I could love him unconditionally, like I wanted to. We still had a long way to go.

I should have bet big bucks that Smokie was going to call me as soon as he got to town. Smokie did get back to town before Julian. My phone rang at about 7:00pm on Monday evening.

"Hello, black beauty! I told Julian I would call and check on you as soon as I got back to town. Are you doing all right?"

I started laughing and said, "Smokie, I thought I told you it wasn't necessary for you to call me for Julian, even if he asked you to." Nothing ever phased Smokie. I don't even know if he was listening to me.

"Look here Shelby, I'm still mad at you for not introducing me to your sister when she was in town. I heard she was fine! I knew that there had to be some more like you at home. Since you can't get with me, the least you could do is hook a brother up with your people."

Smokie was a good-looking man, but I wouldn't fix him up with friend or foe.

"Smokie you already have more women then any man should have. You know I'm not going to fix you up with my sister."

He laughed and told me he wasn't asking me to fix him up. He just wanted me to introduce him to her. He could do all of the "fixing" himself.

"A brother don't need for you to do anything but introduce him. Once she meets me it won't take long for us to do a little 'sumthin, sumthin.' You know what I'm sayin?"

I knew we couldn't have a decent conversation. I was going to hang up before he made me mad.

"Uh, uh! Smokie, you're nasty! Do you think that you're all that and that every woman you meet wants to go to bed with you? If you do, then something is wrong with you and I don't even want to hear about it! Anyway, my sister is not like the women you're used to being with. She doesn't sleep with singers and their entourage. Good night Smokie!"

Smokie laughed at me and said, "Next time your people are in town I can show you better than I can tell you. I got it going on like that! You have a good night too Shelby! I'm just getting back to town and my little freaks didn't come to see me while I was on the road, so I got some business to take care of."

Then he hung up.

I was so pissed that I didn't know what I was going to do. More then anything else I was mad because Smokie talked about what he wanted to do with my sister and because he hung up after calling me a "freak." Well, it sounded like he was calling me one anyway. Julian and I were going to have to have a talk when he got back to town.

CHAPTER
10

*J*ulian arrived on a later flight and called me as soon as he got back. He said his plane landed at about 8:46pm and that there were people all over the place. It was amazing to be a part of his life at this time and see his career blowing up so beautifully. It briefly flashed through my mind that one day I might be crowded out by his fame, nah, just a passing thought. Julian wanted me to come right over. Actually, he was calling from his limo and he wanted to swing by and pick me up, but that would mean that I'd have to spend the night at his house. That was out of the question. I knew what would happen this time if I spent the night! I had talked with Julian three or four times this week and it had only been two weeks since the last time I saw him, but I missed him like I hadn't seen him for the entire two months he was gone.

I got dressed and drove to Julian's house to meet him. When I arrived he hugged me like I had been lost and we were reuniting for the first time in years. He was so strong and smelled so good. I melted at the thought of him holding me. When we kissed I cried. I couldn't think of any other place that I wanted to be at that very moment. I wanted to be right where I was for the rest of my life, but unfortunately real life ain't even like that. We spent the night talking about how well his first concert tour had gone, how much we had missed each other, how groupies act, and the things that his crew did while they were on the road. Before I knew it, it was 1:00am and I needed to get home. The next day was a workday for me. Fortunately, Julian didn't pressure me about staying, he told me he'd pick me up at my house the next evening around 7:00pm. I asked him what he had planned, but he wouldn't tell me. Said it was a surprise. He walked me out to my car and kissed me good night and I sped off.

The next day couldn't go by fast enough. I didn't talk with Julian all day, but I talked with Kyme and Tracie for about 30 minutes after I got home from work. I called Tracie and then called Kyme on my three-way. We talked about what my surprise was going to be. Tracie and Kyme seemed to think that Julian was going to ask me to marry him, but I really didn't think he was going to do that. Actually, I didn't even get my hopes up. I hadn't even told the man I loved him yet. When my doorbell rang I was almost ready to go, so I hung up the phone, ran to the door, opened it, gave Julian a kiss, and told him to have a seat while I put my lipstick on. Instead, he followed me into the bathroom to watch me. He stood behind me and wrapped his arms around my waist and kissed me on the back of my neck.

"Julian, how do you expect me to do this with you kissing me?"

He stopped, and while looking at our reflection in the mirror said, "I don't care if you don't put any lipstick on, you're beautiful without it!"

Then he kissed me on the back of my neck again.

While we were in the car I tried to get Julian to tell me where he was taking me, but he wouldn't cooperate.

He looked over at me and asked, "You like poetry and jazz, right?"

"Of course, I do. Why?"

He never answered me, so that made me anxious to find out where we were going. First, we went to dinner though. While we were eating I kept catching Julian staring at me, so I finally asked.

"What are you staring at? Do I have some food on my face or something?"

He shook his head and said, "I like looking at you, you're beautiful."

I blushed because I didn't know what to say. "Oh, thank you..."

After dinner we headed for Julian's favorite little coffee house, Songs of Solomon. When we arrived, we parked the car in the VIP section and walked in holding hands. Julian found us a table that was situated in the center of the restaurant, a few feet from the front. The lights were very dim, so most of the people that saw us come in didn't seem to recognize him. We ordered coffee and listened to the poem that was being read. I was always amazed by the amount of untapped talent in these kinds of places. Every single poem that was read moved me. It wasn't long before a very handsome guy with dreadlocks was introduced. The name of his poem was, I've Known Your Love All Along." As he begin to read he made eye contact with me and kind of bowed his head a little:

I've Known Your Love All Along

I felt the heat from your gaze across the room
When I turned to see your face your smile
embraced my soul

When you said hello, I heard a melody that
sounded just like love and the movement of your lips
was fluid and smooth

Memories of our love ran through my mind --
warm breezes, setting suns, love, tears, sleepless
nights, smiles, kisses, passion...hot
And all of this...before I even knew your name

Baby, that's what I call you now, you have me sprung
on the honey of your kisses and the rhythm in your

hips
And that same fluid and smooth movement of your
lips...
When you call out my name

So now I hold you in my arms and every night I hold
you even closer in my dreams
I've felt the warmth of your body and I know
intimately the curve of your spine
I've known all along your heat, your honey, your
rhythm, your rhyme, and your sweet, sweet melody
that definitely gets sweeter each time...that you make
me feel that your love is all mine

Girl, it ain't no secret that I love you and I want you in
my life forever, everybody knows that
It's the memories of our love that I've known all along
that I want to share with you

It's the memory of hearing you say, "I love you"
because I've known it all along

I've known your love all along

A piano and a tenor sax accompanied the poem. The
music was almost as beautiful as the poem itself. While the
poem was being read Julian grabbed my right hand and
kissed it. I was thinking that this guy's lady friend must be

very special, so I looked around the room to see if I could find her sitting at a table alone. When I turned around he was standing in front of our table and he handed me a beautifully wrapped box and a dozen peach roses.

"For you!"

I looked at Julian, then I looked back at the guy standing there. Baffled, I looked back at Julian again, with tears in my eyes.

Julian smiled at me and said, "It's for you baby. I love you. It wasn't enough for me to tell you. I wanted everybody else to know too."

I took the box and the flowers and gave Julian a kiss. Everybody in the room clapped. When I opened the box I found the original copy of "I've Known Your Love All Along" on parchment, in a beautiful crystal frame. I asked Julian if we could leave because there was really no point in staying after receiving my gift.

When we got out to the parking lot I put my flowers on top of my gift and placed both of them on top of the car. I grabbed Julian by the lapel of his jacket.

"Come here. Thank you for the poem and the flowers. I don't know what you're trying to do, but I think it's working. You make me feel very special. Every time we're together it just seems to get better and better. I hope I can make you as happy as you make me."

When I kissed him this time it was different because in my heart I was saying, "Julian, I love you." Even though I still couldn't bring myself to say the words out loud.

CHAPTER

11

$\mathscr{I}$ was really surprised when I got to work one day and found a phone mail message from my ex-husband. I hadn't really talked with him since the divorce hearing. While I was listening to his message I thought, "It sounds like he's been drinking." I didn't know what the call was all about, but after thinking about it a little while I came to the conclusion that he definitely had been drinking because the message was left at 1:30am in the morning. It made me kind of sick to my stomach to think that my ex would call me while he was drinking. I didn't know if the call meant he was asking for help, missing me, mad at me, or if he was horny. Who knows? I wasn't going to worry about it though. I didn't need more drama in my life. My hands were full with Julian.

My day went by without incident and there were no more calls from Lorenz, my ex. He probably spent the whole day feeling bad about leaving the message. I was glad that he didn't call to apologize. I didn't feel like hearing it. I had hoped that my head would be pretty clear when I saw Julian that evening. I didn't know what his calendar looked like, but I was going to invite him to ride home with me, for a four day weekend, to meet my parents. It was no big deal because if he couldn't go Tracie and Kyme would make themselves available to take the ride with me. As soon as I was finished at work I called Julian to let him know that I was on my way to his house. We had decided the night before that we would meet for an early dinner. Actually, it would be dinner at a normal time for a change. If he wasn't there when I got there then I'd have a glass of wine and wait...patiently. Miss Gladys was certain to be there, so I could always sit and chitchat with her.

Julian wasn't there when I called and he didn't get home until an hour after I arrived. So, while I waited Miss Gladys and I sat and talked. She was one of the sweetest women I'd ever met. I thought it was really sweet that she felt it was her duty, no, not her duty, but maybe more appropriately, her responsibility to tell me how to treat Julian because he was like a grandson to her. Of course, she was only sharing this information with me because she knew Julian cared about me and as she put it, "I seemed to be a nice girl." Miss Gladys said the worst thing that I could do was to try to take advantage of Julian's kindness. I could see how that would be easy to do because Julian didn't believe in holding back. If he felt like doing something, he did it and if he felt like saying something, he said it. You always knew where he was coming from. The last thing Miss Gladys said to me before Julian came home was, if I hurt him she would make it her business to keep me away from him! It sounded as if that nice, little, old lady was threatening me? I had to admit it was kind of cute.

By the time Julian and I finished dinner it was after 8:00pm. During dinner I asked Julian about going to see my parents. Unfortunately, he had to go out of town for at least a week. He had to leave on Friday morning. I wasn't that disappointed because I knew his schedule was peculiar. Traveling was a large part of his career. Julian assured me that he would make time real soon to meet my folks.

After dinner we lay on the couch in Julian's entertainment room and watched a movie. Lying up against his chest felt really good and when he threw his arm around me and palmed my stomach it felt even better. It wasn't long before Julian was whispering in my ear.

"Shelby, tell me why you make me so happy? What do you do to me girl?"

I laughed and said, "You're silly. I don't do anything to you. It's all in your mind."

Julian said uh, uh and started singing, "Tell me where you came from and when you're going to take me there? You know there's nothing I wouldn't do for you."

He started kissing my ear and the back of my neck. I turned my head, so that I could taste his kisses. Without even thinking about it I rolled over on my back and before I knew it Julian was on top of me. I liked the way the weight of his body felt. Whether he knew it or not he was in control again. I felt Julian's hand run up and down the outside of my thigh. It had been a long time since I'd had the pleasure of feeling anything like that. When he put his hand on the small of my back I thought I was going to lose my mind! I snapped back to reality when Julian said, "Stay with me tonight."

Okay, I didn't know how I was going to get out of this situation. Julian was on top of me, his hand was around my waist, and he was asking me to spend the night with him. The easiest thing to do was to ask him to stop, so I did.

"Julian we better stop."

I tried to push him off of me, but I don't know if I was really trying to get Julian off of me or if I was just going through the motions. I had to make Julian stop before things went too far. This time I said it a little louder and with a little more force.

"Julian please, stop!"

He didn't stop right away, instead he said, "Baby, nothing will change if you don't leave tonight. Stay here with me."

Julian had no idea how much I wanted to stay. I hadn't even had a chance to talk with him about the call from Lorenz.

I found myself pushing him off of me and saying, "Get off of me Julian! I'm not staying!"

Julian stopped, looked at me, and slowly stood up. He put his hand over his mouth and chin, sighed and said, "I'm sorry..."

He walked across the room and stood with his back to me as his hands held the back of his head. I sat up and tightly closed my eyes to keep from crying.

"Maybe I should leave?"

Julian didn't even make a sound, he sort of threw his head back in his hands a little further.

When I finally stood up I slid my shoes on, but I couldn't remember where my purse was. My head was in a fog as I walked around looking for it. I wanted to hurry and leave just so this would be over, but I also wanted to stay and hold Julian. I wanted to let him know that it wouldn't always be like this and that I knew how hard it was for him because it was hard for me too! After I found my purse on the kitchen counter I went back to let Julian know I was leaving. When I found him he was sitting on the couch looking at the TV.

I walked into the room and softly said, "I'm going to leave now."

He said okay and got up to walk me to the door. We walked to the door in an uncomfortable silence. I wondered what he was thinking about. When I opened the door we both stood there for a few seconds and looked at my car. I gathered my thoughts and turned around to face Julian.

"Can I get a good night hug?"

As I asked for a hug I reached for him. I'm pretty sure he only hugged me back because I was hugging him. The strength and firmness of his hug surprised me. I closed my eyes and laid my head against his chest. I managed to softly say that I was sorry.

Julian cradled my head with his hand and said, "Yea, I know, me too..."

When I looked up at him he gently held my face and kissed me on my forehead.

Then he said, "Good night baby."

I gave him a half smile and told him that I'd call him. He shook his head okay.

After I started my car and drove down the street a short distance, I pulled over and rested my forehead on the steering wheel. Maybe I was asking this man for too much. He could hold me, kiss me, hug me, and love me, but no matter how excited he got I wasn't going to let him make love to me! I wondered if I was being reasonable? I thought that maybe the answer might have been to break things off. I had to stop and take a look at myself, sitting there making what could be considered a major life decision on the side of the road. When I got home I immediately checked my answering machine ... no Julian. I took a quick shower and dressed for bed. As I walked toward my bed I looked at the phone and wondered if I should call him. By the time I crawled under the covers I decided I should call because we needed to talk while things were still fresh on our minds. Julian's phone rang several times. All kinds of thoughts ran through my head, "Maybe he called someone over to relieve the pressure, or maybe he had gone over to another woman's house?" When he did pick up the phone he sounded like he had been sleeping (that never crossed my mind).

"I'm sorry Julian, did I wake you up?"

He said, "No, I'm glad you called."

Well, it made me feel a little better to know that he was still speaking to me.

I took a deep breath and started talking, "I'm sorry about what happened earlier tonight. I let things go too far and I shouldn't have done that. I really feel like we need to talk about it."

At first he didn't say anything, then, "You're right, we do need to talk about it. First of all though, I want to apologize to you because I lost it for a few minutes! Like I said before, I know nothing would have changed if you had stayed tonight, but of course nothing's going to change because you didn't stay either. I know you want to wait until we're married to make love. Baby, I can't do anything but respect that. I wish I could promise you that I won't get mad or frustrated about it though. I guess you just have to teach me how to be patient. This is brand new to me. I've never had to wait before."

Julian had surprised me again! I thought for sure that he was going to say let's not see each other for a while. I was glad that he apologized, but something was wrong because I was still a little sad.

"Baby, I know that this is really hard for you because it's hard for me too. I feel like I'm asking you for too much. If you want to see other people I'll understand. Our relationship would have to change of course, but having you in my life has meant so much at this point that I'm willing to hold on to our friendship any way that I can. I want you to be happy Julian. I know our relationship isn't based on sex, but if that's something that's really important to you ..."

Before I could say another word Julian laughed and told me to stop, "Shelby, just stop okay. I think you're being a little dramatic about this. I'd like to believe that I'm a little deeper than that. You mean a lot more to me than just sex. Over the last few years I've met a lot of women who've wanted to be a part of my life because of the things that I've acquired. Most of the women that I've had in my life didn't really want me. The very first day that I saw you I knew I was going to love you. When you smiled at me I knew that you were going to love me back. I could tell that you were going to bring something to my life that I was missing. I guess what I'm saying is, if I have to wait another lifetime to make love to you, then I guess I'll just have to wait. To be honest with you, I find waiting kind of sexy. Girl, we'll be all right! If this is the biggest problem that we ever have then we don't have any problems. Right?"

Everything that Julian said made me love him even more, so I agreed with what he said.

"Since you put it like that, I guess you're right. I should start worrying when I find something to worry about, huh?"

Everything seemed to be okay for the moment.

Julian interrupted my thought by saying, If we're all straight now, I think I'm going to go to bed because 'not' making love to you has worn me out."

I laughed and told him he was silly. We said good night and as usual Julian asked for a good night kiss to help him sleep. I guess everything was going to be all right after all.

CHAPTER
12

$\mathcal{A}$ couple of days went by before I went over to Julian's again. I had to work on my self-control. On that particular day Smokie showed up with a girl, well a very attractive woman, who's skirt was so short that if she bent over I would have gotten to know her personally. If she had sneezed her breast would have fallen out of her little blouse. She was Julian's ex, so it didn't take a rocket scientist to know that she was going to be trouble. As they walked into the entertainment room Smokie announced their presence.

"Hey Shelby baby! Ju'man, look who I found outside? Camilla the man killa!" Then he started laughing.

She never even looked at me when she very dryly said, "Hello…" She immediately turned her attention to Julian who was sitting next to me. "Julian I need to talk to you…now!"

I turned and looked at him as if to say, I know she's not coming in here ordering people around and I know you're getting ready to show her the door.

Julian stood up and said, "Shell, I'll be right back."

Then he walked out of the room with "Camilla the man killa…"

Smokie loved every minute of whatever had just happened.

As he sat down next to me he said, "You trust her with your man, huh? She ain't no joke and talk about a freak. They don't come no freakier. It ain't no secret that I've had a piece of that. Look here girlfriend, you need to get with the program. Go ahead and hook my brother Ju'man up with some of yo' lovin'. I know you capable 'cause you built like a prize winning quarter horse. Then you need to come on over and let Smokie love you down. I promise you won't be disappointed. Look at Camilla, she can't stay away from here."

He laughed so hard, I thought he was going to have an asthma attack! I sat there and looked at him because I couldn't believe that he was tripping like that. The more I thought about it the madder I got, so instead of saying anything to him (because it wouldn't have meant anything to him anyway) I got up to go see what was taking Julian so long. When I stood up, Smokie stood up too. He went over to the bar and fixed himself a drink.

He looked over at me and said, "You need a drink sweetheart? If my man was by his self with Camilla I'd be on it!"

He started laughing as he lifted his drink up to his lips. The more he laughed the madder I got.

I looked over at him and said, "Smokie, something is wrong with you. You aren't right, but you know that, don't you? Sometime you just make me sick, you really make me sick."

I knew that Smokie wasn't paying any attention to what I said, so I left the room to look for my man.

I didn't know what to expect when I did find Julian and Camilla, but I knew Julian wouldn't disappoint me...I hoped! I went to the kitchen and they weren't there. Actually, I didn't think that they would be. I went through the dining room to get to the living room and I finally heard them in the foyer. I could hear Julian telling Camilla that she needed to leave and he would talk with her later, but she was crying and wanted to know why he wouldn't talk with her then. I couldn't believe that she was in his house tripping like that while I was there. I thought to myself, "I'm going to have to bust this up because girlfriend is going to give me my respect! Julian is being way too nice for me, so I have to make my presence known."

Just as I was about to walk into the foyer I heard Julian say, "Come on now Camilla! It hasn't been like that in a long time. That doesn't work anymore!"

She was still crying when I heard her respond, "But baby, you know I need you! Let's just go up to your room. You know how good I used to make you feel. Nothing has changed. I can make you forget about Sheila or whatever her name is! I can make you feel better then she does."

Okay, it was time for me to intervene. Enough was enough! I walked into the foyer.

"Julian, what's going on? Is everything all right out here?"

Camilla's arms were up around Julian's neck and Julian was wrestling to get her hands off of him. When they realized that I was there everything stopped, Camilla's arms dropped down to her side, and she turned her head so that I couldn't see that she was crying. I walked over to Julian and put my arm around his waist and looked at Camilla.

"I'm sorry, is there something that I can help you with Camilla? You look upset."

She glared at me and said, "You can't do a thing for me! Julian, I'll talk with you later!"

Then she stormed out the door and sped off in her car. She never looked back. I was so pissed I didn't know what to do! The first thing I did though was to take my arm from around Julian's waist, then I turned and looked at him.

"What was up with her? I mean, what was that all about?"

Julian looked kind of agitated when he said, "Look baby, I really don't want to talk about it right now!"

He started walking away and I thought, Excuse me! I don't care how you feel, you need to tell me something!

I grabbed his arm and said, "Uhm, excuse me Julian, but some half naked woman comes into your home while I'm here and tries to talk you into going to bed with her. I don't know what you would say about that, but I say that she disrespected me. Then you tell me that you don't want to talk about it right now? Uh, uh...no!"

Julian turned and looked at me and said, "Look, I don't need you tripping on me too! You either trust me or you

don't. Either way, I don't want to talk about it right now!"
As he turned to walk away I heard him say under his breath,
"Women are a trip!"

Well, since he wasn't going to talk about it and he was
headed back to the entertainment room I guess that was
supposed to be the end of it, but it was far from being over.
I didn't want to continue this in front of Smokie because I
knew he would only make matters worse.

When I walked into the entertainment room I could
tell Smokie was ready to start some more trouble.

"Where's Camilla? Did you give her the boot Shelby?"
I acted like I didn't hear him.

Julian responded, "Man, don't let her in my house anymore. She's even crazier then she was when we were kickin
it!" Julian fixed himself a drink and then looked at me, "You
want one?"

I shook my head and sat down across the room from
Smokie. I looked at Smokie as I bit my bottom lip and
thought, "He knew what he was doing when he let her in.
This isn't going to work. I don't want Smokie around when
I'm with Julian. He disrupts our flow!" While I was looking
at Smokie he blew me a kiss! I sighed and turned my head.
"I can't figure him out!" It was as good a time as any to
leave because I wanted to talk about Camilla and I wasn't
going to do it with Smokie there, so I stood up to leave.

"Julian, you know what? I think I'm going to go
home."

Julian grabbed me by my hand as I walked past him.

"Baby, don't leave, I want you to stay."

I looked at him and then I looked at Smokie. Julian knew what I was trying to say, so he asked Smokie to leave.

"Man, don't you have somewhere you're supposed to be?"

Smokie smiled and said, "Nah, I want to stay here with y'all!" As he stood up he said, "Yea I do, matter of fact, if I drive fast enough I might be able to catch up with your girl."

As Julian pulled me close to him he said, "That ain't funny man!"

As soon as I thought Smokie was gone I asked Julian, "Why did Smokie do that?"

Julian looked at me all puzzled like he didn't know what I was talking about. "Do what? What did my boy do?"

I stepped back and looked at him. "Smokie knew I was here and he brought that woman in the house anyway."

Julian looked at me like I was crazy and said, "How was Smokie supposed to know you were here? Aren't you parked around back? And why would he do anything to disrespect you Shelby? He knows you're my lady and he knows how I feel about you. I can't believe you're tripping like this! I know what you're really mad about...Camilla. Let me assure you, she won't be coming over here anymore! You heard me tell Smokie not to let her in my house again and tomorrow I'll tell her that she's not welcome over here. Problem solved!"

Julian had not made me feel any better. As a matter of

fact, I had gotten a little more upset. He was acting like this whole situation with Smokie and Camilla was no big deal!

"Wait, wait, wait! First of all, why has that freak been coming over here anyway? Second of all, what's up with Smokie? He told me that he had slept with her. Excuse me if I sound confused, but if you were dating her, what was Smokie doing have sex with her? Is that something y'all do often, share women? 'Cause if it is, I'm not the one! Plus, I don't like Smokie always trying to pull up on me! If he's your boy and everything, then you need to tell him to stop! Sometimes he really makes me feel uncomfortable and I'm getting to a point where I don't want him around when I'm with you!"

Julian shook his head and pretty much told me to stop tripping because he wasn't going to make a choice between Smokie and me.

"Whoa baby! That's just Smokie! I've already told you that Smokie is not going to disrespect you because you are 'my lady!' But just so it's clear, if I'm with a woman and she does get it on with my boy, she can't be my lady anymore! Hence, the story of Camilla... And as far as who comes to my house is concerned, this is my house and I can handle myself. I'm not going to disrespect you because I love you, plain and simple!"

Both of us just stood there for what seemed like forever, but it was only a few seconds.

Finally I said, "Look, you're upset and I'm upset, so I'm going to leave. I need the fresh air anyway. This whole scene tonight is messing with my head!"

As I turned to leave the room Julian grabbed me, "Baby, you don't need to leave and anyway I want you to stay."

I shook my head and said, "Uh, uh...I need to go."

Julian sighed and said, "Okay...but can I at least get a kiss before you leave me?"

I looked at him and said, "I shouldn't..."

Julian smiled and said, "But we both know you want to!"

We kissed and then he held my hand as he walked me to my car. When we got to the car I turned and faced him. "Don't fool me Julian."

Julian put his hands on my waist and right before he kissed me again he said, "I can 't fool you Miss Simone, I love you!"

I looked in my rearview mirror as I drove down the drive and I could see Julian watching me as I pulled away.

It took me about three days to finally get over the scene at Julian's house. Tracie knew something was wrong with me, but she's not one to put pressure on me. I eventually told Tracie and Kyme about Camilla.

All Tracie could say was "Deg!" Then she would stop, look at me and say it again, "Deg!" Kyme was ready to find out where Camilla lived so she could tell her how much of a tramp she was...and she had never even met the woman.

Tracie looked at me with her face twisted and asked, "So what you gonna do? I take it you haven't talked with Julian in a couple of days? What y'all gonna do?"

Kyme jumped right in, "What is Julian's phone number? I want to talk with him! What is his problem? I can't believe he let some woman trip like that while you were there! Give me the telephone. He is not going to have other women disrespecting you. If she's an ex-girlfriend then she needs to get out of the picture!"

I looked at Kyme and told her to get over it because I was. I had a couple of days to think about it and I came to the conclusion that Camilla was just an irate, ex-girlfriend that Julian really didn't have anything to do with. Julian and I were still going to have to talk about women coming to his house, particularly when I'm not there. Actually, I don't want them there when I'm there either!

Now, Smokie. I still couldn't figure out what his problem was. Sometimes I really liked him and sometimes I couldn't stand him! I made up my mind to talk with Julian about him too. I didn't know how it was going to turn out, but I knew I had to at least let him know how I felt.

Tracie gave me the best advice. "You know, Julian hasn't called you because he thinks you're still mad with him. Why don't you call him and invite him over? Just think, y'all will be on neutral ground, no Smokie, no other women! Girl, you don't need me to tell you what to do. I don't have a man."

We got a laugh out of that, but she was right, I needed to call Julian to let him know that I wasn't upset. While they were still at my house I called him. The whole time he and I talked Kyme and Tracie made faces at me. They are such teenagers sometimes. It was good to hear his voice. I could tell that he was smiling and that made me happy. He's such a busy fella. We made plans to meet on Friday for dinner at my place.

After I hung up the phone I was grinning so much that Tracie said, "Ooh, he must have said something mighty, mighty good!"

I laughed at her and said, "No, I just thought about something. We're going to have dinner on Friday and Thursday is our one-year anniversary. It's been a whole year since we first met."

Even though Kyme liked Julian I guess she was still a little upset by the incident with Camilla.

She looked at me and said, "I guess you're going to do something special...for the occasion I mean?"

I smiled, "No, just dinner, but I think I'll go and get him a gift tomorrow during lunch. What do you think I should get him?"

Kyme looked at me and rolled her eyes, "I don't know, maybe some kind of restraint!"

CHAPTER

13

I didn't get a chance to talk with Julian on Thursday because he had to fly out of town for a few radio interviews. When he got back it was late, so he didn't call me, but the first voice that I heard when I woke up on Friday morning was his. He called and woke me up for work.

"Good morning baby girl, are you up yet?"

I smiled, "No, but good morning anyway! What are you doing up so early?"

Julian told me that he wanted to be the first one to say good morning to me and he wanted to tell me about the date he was going on that evening. He told me the lady he was meeting was a beautiful, tall, black, Amazonian princess. I asked him if she was good to him?

He laughed and said, "She's the best thing that has happened in my life in years."

So I asked, "If she's so good to you, why isn't she your queen?"

He laughed and said, "She's not my queen yet because she hasn't married me. After we're married she'll be the queen of my everything."

Knowing him and loving him sometimes felt like make believe. He's exactly the kind of guy that you dream of meeting, even though you think he really doesn't exist. We agreed to have dinner at 7:00pm and Julian promised he wouldn't be late.

My workday went by without incident. It was a pretty dull day. During lunch I met Tracie and she helped me pick out an anniversary gift for Julian. I needed help because I couldn't imagine what to get the man. He has enough money to get anything he wants. We ended up picking out a very nice silk robe with a pair of matching boxers. On the way home from work I picked up some fresh asparagus, chicken divan, a mushroom vinaigrette salad, and of course I got us a couple of bottles of wine. Even though Julian doesn't eat a lot of sweets, I bought a small German chocolate cheesecake for desert.

It was hard to believe that it had been a whole year since I first met Julian. It had also been a whole year since my divorce. I wondered how Lorenz was doing. If he had been doing bad I'm sure I would have heard from his mom. After my ex-husband and I separated she would call to tell me that she missed me...and that he missed me too! For months she tried to convince me that her son couldn't make it without me. I didn't want to be the one to tell her that her son was a drunk and a womanizer. As far as I was concerned, he had everything he needed. The last time I talked with her I told her that I had met a very nice man that I was "very" happy with, so there was no chance that Lorenz and

I would be getting back together...ever. I wished Lorenz the best that life had to offer. Even though she was hurt she understood that I couldn't ... wouldn't wait on Lorenz to get his life together. Her calls stopped.

Julian and I had come from meeting each other at a restaurant, to seeing each other on an almost daily basis. It was hard to believe that it had only been one year. Time had really flown. I thought the relationship was progressing at a nice pace, not to fast and not to slow. I thought, "Maybe by this time next year I'll be Mrs. Julian Brishard." I liked the way that sounded.

When Julian arrived he was gorgeous! He had on a raised print, semi-sheer, red shirt, with the two top buttons open, black slacks, and a silver chain. I loved his shoes too. They were black lace ups, with a strap that buckled across the laces. The boy really has good taste in clothes. When I opened the door he held up two dozen white tulips and said happy anniversary! See, that's what I meant, what other man would remember the anniversary of your meeting each other? And not only had he remembered our anniversary, but he also brought my favorite flowers. I gave him a great big ole' kiss, grabbed him by the hand, and pulled him in the door. I hurried in the kitchen to get a vase for my flowers, so that I could move the candles off of the dinner table. Julian made himself comfortable to Mint Condition playing in the living room.

As he shook his head and bit his bottom lip he said, "If I didn't know any better I would think you were trying to seduce a brother. You're pretty smooth Shelby Simone, wine chilling, music playing, scented candles burning, gotcha' little black, lace dress on. Yea, you tryin' to mess a brother's head up. That's what you're doing. You know I'm right."

I brought Julian a glass of wine and sat down next to him on the couch. We talked for about 30 minutes. I could have sat there listening to him all night, but instead we got up and had dinner. After dinner I asked Julian if he wanted dessert.

"No, looking at you is like having dessert, sweet, dark, chocolate."

I laughed and hit his hand, "You are a smooth talker."

After dinner we went back into the living room and sat on the couch. I gave him his gift and watched him smile as he opened it. He pulled the robe out of the box and held it up, then he pulled the boxers out and held them up too.

He looked at me and said, "Thank you baby! How did you know what size I wore?"

The robe and boxers were a red, black, and dark gold paisley print. As he held them up I imagined how good he was going to look in them. He must have been reading my mind.

"I can't wait to show you how good I look in them."

I smiled, but didn't respond. He took his hands and gently placed them on either side of my face and kissed me.

"Thank you for another perfect night! Oh, wait a minute."

He pulled a little jewelry box from his pocket, "This

must be for you."

He handed me the little, black, velvety box and watched me as I slowly opened it. It was a pair of two-carat diamond, stud earrings. My heart almost led me to believe that it was going to be an engagement ring. The earrings were beautiful though. I was really surprised and he knew it. I hugged him and kissed him all over his face. He held me and told me how much he loved me.

"You know Shell, I've never felt this way about anybody before. Everything about this, us, has been new to me. Thank you for dinner tonight and thank you for letting me into your life. If you had said no that first night things would have been very different. You might have been sitting here with some knucklehead. What do you think we can do to top this next year?"

I looked at him, smiled and gently stroked his cheek. "I don't know, but it's been a good year for me too. After I realized that my marriage was really over, I had no idea that I was going to meet someone like you. It feels good to be happy again. So, thank you. Can I ask you something though? Do you think we'll always be this happy? Never mind, don't answer that. I'd like to believe that we can do this."

Julian left at about 2:00am the next morning.

Before leaving he said, "You sure you don't want me to stay and model my robe for you?"

I smiled mischievously and said," If you put those boxers on I can assure you that Julian Brishard would never want to leave here."

He laughed, "Oh, so you gonna' tease me? That's not fair."

I apologized and told him that my comment was uncalled for, but true. We kissed and said good night. We agreed to meet tomorrow and go to a matinee. It was good to know that after a year the newness of our relationship hadn't worn off.

On Saturday my sisters, Kari and Sharrin called to ask if they could come up and hang out with me in three weeks? Of course I had no problem with that, but I was sure more was involved, so I asked.

"Kari, what are y'all really coming up here for?"

Kari laughed and said, "Because you are our baby sister and we love you and miss you and we want to see you!"

I knew that wasn't it, so I asked again, "Okay, I'm going to ask one more time. What is the real reason that y'all are coming up here? It wouldn't have anything to do with Julian would it?"

I only asked that because Kari usually traveled with her husband and her kids. She didn't leave them behind too often.

Finally Sharrin broke down. "Kari wants to meet Julian! But why can't we be coming up there to check on you? You act like we don't love you or something?"

I laughed and told them I knew that they loved me. I figured, if Coco could come to town and hang out with my boyfriend, then what's to make me think my sisters wouldn't do the same thing? Coco had actually come to town on two or three occasions with some of his boys and hung out with Julian, clubbing and partying. The only reason I even knew Coco was in town was because Julian called me and told me he was at his house. So, now Kari and Sharrin were coming to visit. I would have to ask Julian if we could stay at his place for that weekend. I'm sure he wouldn't have a problem with it. He probably would be very excited about entertaining more of my family.

I decided to make it a girls' weekend at Julian's house. I invited Tracie and Kyme to hang out with us.

The first thing Kyme said was, "You do realize this is the first time that you've asked us to a party at Julian's.

"Yea...and your point is?"

There were times when Kyme just pissed me off and I felt like this was going to be one of those times.

"What's your point Kyme?"

She felt like the only reason I was inviting them was because my sisters were going to be in town and I felt guilty. I told her that she was being ridiculous.

"Anyway Kyme, we're talking about staying at Julian's home, not some summer resort! Give me a break! Y'all visit out there all of the time. We even go out there to work out sometimes. So, what's the big deal? I didn't think you were into that whole party thing anyway?"

She was going to make her point whatever it was, "Shell, all I'm saying is, if you had really wanted us to go to any parties out there, you would have invited us before now."

If Kyme only knew! It's torture for me to be at Julian's house all night, whether other people are there or not. I love him and we have some crazy sexual tension going on. Hanging out with him like that does nothing but create more tension and frustration between us.

I finally conceded and said, "Yea, you're right Kyme...I never thought about it like that. I should have been more sensitive. So are you going or not?"

Tracie, who had been sitting there listening the whole time said, "I don't know what Kyme is tripping about. I'm already there!"

Sharrin and Kari showed up late on a Friday afternoon, so I took the afternoon off to pick them up from the airport. I already had my clothes packed, so we wouldn't need to go by my house. Tracie and Kyme were going to meet us at Julian's house at around 6:30pm or 7:00pm. On the way to Julian's I asked about my niece and nephews and about Sharrin's boyfriend, who she claimed was "just a friend." Kari looked good for a 38-year-old with three kids. She could easily pass for 25. My sisters are some beautiful women.

When we arrived at Julian's house Kari said she was impressed. She quickly qualified what she was saying by explaining that it wasn't his wealth that she was impressed with, but that such a young man was doing so well for himself. I understood exactly what she was saying because one thing that I always admired about my oldest sister was that she was not a materialistic person, not the least bit pretentious...never was. I remembered when guys would come by the house to take her out. My mom and dad didn't have to check them out because by the time Kari finished with them, if they came by to impress her with their car, jewelry, or clothes, she would have them nearly in tears as they left the house. She is definitely a "no nonsense" kind of gal!

I love her and I've learned so much from her through the years. I really have a lot of respect for her.

Sharrin, on the other hand, is the "party" sister. She and Coco are most alike, even though she and Collin are the twins. Sharrin is always looking for a party! It would stand to reason that she would be the one dating Julian instead of me. She loves rubbing elbows with the entertainers and the blue bloods of society. When we were growing up, she, in fact, was the one that was impressed by the clothes, jewelry, and cars. I love Sharrin too and I know that I can always count on having fun when I'm with her. She wouldn't stand for it to be any other way.

I parked the car in the back and we went into the house. Miss Gladys was still there, so I introduced her to Kari and reintroduced her to Sharrin while she was finishing dinner for us. She showed me where the rest of the food was that she had prepared for us for the weekend. She had taken her time and cooked during the week and put the food in the deep freezer for us to thaw out when we got ready for it. Before Miss Gladys left she told us that we were some of the prettiest girls that she had ever seen and for all of us to be careful. She gave us a quick mother daughter talk about men, sex, drugs, alcohol, and staying up all night. Kari told Miss Gladys how old she was and that she was married with three children, and that she would keep us in check. Miss Gladys was surprised to hear that Kari was 38 years old. She went on to say that she wasn't concerned with Julian's behavior, but some of his friends were a little rowdy.

At that point I interjected and said, "Like Smokie…"

Miss Gladys stopped me and said, "Oh no, he's a nice young man! Always so helpful when he's here!"

I grinned at her and asked, "Smokie?"

Miss Gladys shook her head and assured me that Smokie was one of the nicest young men that she knew, right behind Julian.

All I could say was "Uh!"

I escorted Kari and Sharrin upstairs. We had our pick of bedrooms, so I chose the one farthest from Julian's. I was trying to fool myself into believing that the distance between the bedrooms was going to somehow make a difference. It had been two years since the last time I was with Lorenz. I was a big girl. I was sure I could handle myself. In the mean time, Sharrin was ready to get the party started. I could hear her down the hall.

"Shelby, what time is Julian getting here and what

time is the party starting?"

I screamed back down the hall, "Sharrin chill out, you have all night to party! Julian should be home in a couple of hours. Relax!"

After unpacking we went back downstairs to the kitchen. We decided to postpone eating dinner until Kyme and Tracie showed up. Instead of eating I took Kari on a tour of the house. We went to my favorite room, the entertainment room and my second favorite place, the patio next to the pool.

Kari asked, "Does he live here alone?"

I looked at her, "Yea, why?"

She looked at me with a partial grin, "Shelby, this is a big house for a single man and from all of the videos that I've seen him in, he's pretty good looking. So, I'm asking if you're sure that no other women stay here?"

Even though I didn't appreciate the insinuation, I understood why she was asking, she's just practical like that. I assured her that Julian was not seeing any other women, but that from time to time his friends (men friends) did stay over with their dates, but we were working on changing that.

She shook her head and said, "Oh, okay..."

What now? I thought.

Kari grabbed my hand and asked, "How serious are you about Julian and how serious is he about you? I'm just asking because I don't want you to get hurt. I love you and I know you can handle yourself, but I want to make sure that you're not blinded by the glitz and glamour of his world."

I looked at Kari and smiled. The one thing that I admired most about her was the same thing I disliked most. She didn't beat around the bush and she always had your best interest at heart ... to a fault.

I looked at her and said, "Kari, when I met Julian I had no idea who he was for about a week and by the end of the first month I liked him anyway. I've done a lot of thinking about this relationship. He respects me and he treats me very well. We've been together for a year and he understands that I'm going to be celibate until I'm married. So, it's not like he's taking advantage of me. I think I'm in love with him! He is just so good to me...and for me. We're good for each other. When you meet him you'll see what I'm talking about. I guarantee you'll like him, watch and see."

Kari gave me a hug and said, "If you love him then I know he can't be too bad. Just be careful!"

We made our way back to the kitchen and found that Sharrin had fixed herself a plate. She said she was hungry and couldn't wait another minute. Kyme and Tracie were coming in the back door, so I took them upstairs to unload their luggage. We went back downstairs and had some dinner. Well, all of us except Kyme. Tracie said she told Kyme that we were all going to have dinner together at Julian's, but Kyme couldn't wait. She stopped on the way and picked up something to eat. That girl can be so difficult sometimes. If she wasn't my friend I really don't think I would be bothered with her one minute. While we were having dinner

Julian walked in.

"Well, this is what I like to come home to, a house full of beautiful women!"

I got up, walked over to him, and gave him a kiss. Then I introduced him to Kari. He shook her hand and gave her a hug.

"It's nice meeting you Kari. Shelby has told me some really nice things about you. Please make yourself at home while you're here."

He looked at everybody and said it again, "Actually, that goes for all of you, make yourselves at home. You are not considered guests here."

Sharrin looked over at Julian and said, "So brother-in-law what time does the party start?"

He looked at his watch and back up at Sharrin and told her that the party wouldn't start until about 10:00pm or 11:00pm. He told us to relax until then. I walked upstairs with Julian to ask him who was coming. He told me that it would be the regulars and Smokie. I had forgotten all about Smokie. I guess everybody would get a chance to meet the "infamous" Smokie.

After I showered and finished getting dressed I went into everybody else's room to see what they were wearing. Kari was wearing a pair of black hip huggers with a sheer black blouse and a lacy black camisole underneath. Sharrin on the other hand was wearing a little red, spaghetti strapped dress, some red stockings, and a pair of 3 inch red pumps. Kyme was wearing pants too and Tracie was struggling over a cute lime green lace dress or a shiny silver dress. I voted on the lime green dress. I had on a long, brown, straight spaghetti strapped dress, with a thin, white stripe down both sides. I was cute I thought! As I was coming out of the room (Tracie and I were sharing a room) Smokie was coming in the living room from the kitchen, making a loud entrance.

"Okay, let's get this party started! I'm ready to get my dance on! Who's here? Shelby, come on downstairs and dance with me."

He looked upstairs and saw me and Kari standing at the top of the staircase. Sharrin also came out of her room to see what all the fuss was.

"Who is that screaming like a crazy person?" Kari wanted to know.

I looked at Smokie, who was standing at the bottom of the staircase and then I looked back at Kari.

"Kari, I'd like to introduce you to the crazy person, Smokie. Smokie this is my sister Kari and my sister Sharrin."

Smokie uttered some explicative and ran up the stairs.

"Y'all must come from a family that doesn't have any ugly people in it? Look at y'all! I feel like a kid in a candy store!"

Kari stopped him, "Let me assist you a little here. I'm married, Shelby is dating Julian, and Sharrin's boyfriend is back home. So you're actually more like a kid in a china shop. Keep your hands in your pocket and don't touch anything!"

Smokie looked down at his feet and started laughing, "I can tell that you and Shelby are sisters. Y'all both have that quick wit that I love so much! Look here, Sharrin save the 'first' and the 'last' dance for me 'cause you working that red dress girl!"

Smokie walked past us and went into Julian's room.

Kari looked back at me, "That can't be the nice young man that Miss Gladys was talking about?"

I shook my head and went on downstairs to the kitchen. I started putting out a few finger foods. Miss Gladys made about 80 trays of hors'douvres. She was wonderful. I was glad that she was around to keep an eye on Julian. All I had to do was show the folks that would be serving during the party where everything was. The bartenders didn't need any help because there were two fully stocked bars that also had nonalcoholic drinks and bottled water. While I was walking around Julian walked up behind me and put his arms around me. I love it when he does that. His arms were so strong. He kissed me on the back of my neck and told me that he was glad that I was there.

"You look good girl! I want y'all to have a good time this weekend. Just let me know if I can do anything for you ladies."

I turned around and looked at him, "You're so sweet! You spoil me boy!"

As we were kissing Smokie walked in.

"What are y'all doing? Oh, I know...y'all must be kissing! Every time I turn around y'all got your lips all over each other. Y'all better watch out! Y'all goin' be in love in a minute."

I didn't even have a smart remark for Smokie because I did love Julian and I didn't want to dispute that. Julian and Smokie left the room and went to the entertainment room to turn on some music. As they were walking out I could hear Smokie talking about Sharrin. I wasn't worried about her because if anybody could handle Smokie she could.

The party was in full swing by 2:30am! I looked around and Kari was talking with D'Angelo and both Kyme and Tracie were busy dancing. I hadn't seen Sharrin in a while, so I took a little walk to look for her. The more I thought about it, the more I realized that I hadn't heard Smokie's mouth in a while either. I went to the kitchen and there were people talking and dancing in there too. I worked my way through the dining room to the entertainment room. Now I was getting a little worried because I really couldn't find Sharrin. I walked out to the patio and there she was dancing with Smokie. A very slow song was playing and they appeared to be doing more talking then dancing. I would never have guessed it, Smokie and Sharrin. Now that I knew she was okay, I started looking for Julian because I hadn't seen him in a while either. When I went back into the house I ran into Tyra Banks, and asked her if she had seen Julian.

She looked at me and said, "Yea, about 10 or 15 minutes ago he was headed upstairs and some woman was right behind him. You better go get your man girlfriend."

I shook my head and headed upstairs.

Julian's bedroom door was open so I walked right in. Camilla was lying on the bed and Julian was leaning up against his dresser, calmly telling her that she had to either leave the room or leave the house. I walked over to Julian and stood next to him.

"Is everything okay?"

He stood up straight and put his arm around me, "Hey babe, I was just telling Camilla that she needed to leave."

I looked at him and motioned for the glass of wine that he had in his hand. I took a sip out of it and looked at Camilla.

"Look dear, I can understand you still wanting to be with Julian, but he's with me now and I don't appreciate that every time I turn around you're up in his face. So, you really do need to take Julian's suggestion and leave. I personally think he's being too kind by giving you a choice, but since this isn't my home, "YET," there's not much I can say about it!"

Julian didn't interrupt me while I was talking. He just stood there and looked at me. When I finished I took another sip out of his glass and handed it back to him. Camilla slowly got up, rolled her eyes at me, and walked out of the room.

As she walked out the door she turned around and said, "Julian, I'm sure I'll talk with you later. You're going to have to tell her about us sooner or later! You might as well tell her now!"

She slammed the door behind her as she made her, oh so, dramatic exit.

Julian put his glass down and stood in front of me. He put his hands on the dresser on either side of me.

"I like the way you took control then. It let's me know that you care...and it was kind of sexy."

I looked up at him, "So, what was she talking about? What is it that you need to tell me?"

He laughed as he started kissing my face, "Nothing! She was just trying to stir you up. That's how she works. If she can keep you mad at me, then she figures she has a chance. Don't fall for it."

He kissed me on my forehead, then my eyes, and then my cheeks, my neck, and then the top of my chest. Then he stopped and kissed me on my lips. He grabbed me by my waist and the next thing I knew he was picking me up and putting me on the bed. I didn't resist. Maybe this was what I had to do to keep him away from Camilla. I was anchored down by the weight of his body on mine and the heat that I felt was feverish. The smell of his cologne alone was about to drive me out of my mind. I was just a little bit too involved to stop now. I didn't want to stop. I rolled over on top of him and started unbuttoning his shirt and kissing his face and his neck and his chest. He had his hands on my thighs, which were straddling him. I could feel my dress going higher and higher up my legs as I kissed him.

I whispered in his ear, "I want to make love to you so bad I could scream."

All he could manage to say was, "Me too."

I started unbuckling his belt. It didn't dawn on either one of us that the door wasn't locked because at that very moment there was a loud knock and it flew open. It was Kari.

"Excuse me, I don't know if either of you is aware of it, but there's a 'party' going on downstairs and if I'm not mistaken, Julian is the host. One of you may want to come downstairs and entertain the guests."

Kari walked out and left the door open. I stopped and rested my forehead on Julian's chin. I took a deep breath and dismounted him. I straightened out my dress and my hair and stood there looking at him pensively. Julian lay there for a moment, then he took his hands and wiped his face.

"You know you're going to drive me crazy girl! I can't take this. I can't take it!"

He sat up on the side of the bed and buttoned his shirt, then he stood up, put his shirt back into his pants, and buckled his belt.

Julian went back downstairs to the party. I took a shower and went to bed. He said I was going to drive him crazy...how did he think I felt? We were just minutes away from having sex. "This has got to stop! This madness has got to stop!" I jumped into bed and grabbed the remote. It was about 3:45am and I couldn't find anything on TV that I wanted to watch. I continued to flip through the channels anyway. There was a knock at the door, so I got up and unlocked it. It was Kari. She came in and shut the door behind her.

"What were you thinking about...getting busy with Julian with a house full of people downstairs? And to top it off, you didn't even bother to lock the door. I would not have thought anything about not seeing you, but some half-naked woman walked by me and was telling somebody that she was leaving and that Julian was up in his bedroom with what's her name." I assumed she was referring to you. I wasn't sure! Look Shelby, what you do is your business, but at least have some respect for yourself. I thought you said y'all were going to wait anyway?"

I sat up on the bed and looked at her, "First of all Kari, you're right, it is my business! Second of all, we were not having sex, and third of all, we just got caught up in the moment. I think we both had a little bit too much to drink." I looked down at the floor, "Kari, I love him so much that it's driving me crazy. I want to make love to him, but I want to wait too. I know he's frustrated because I'm frustrated. These near misses are really getting old. Can I tell you something? The truth is, I almost had sex with him tonight because I thought it might be the thing to do to keep him away from Camilla, that half naked woman that you were talking about."

Kari shook her head, "Girl please, you sound like a six-teen year old. You know it doesn't work like that! Just from the little bit of time that I've spent with Julian I can tell that he loves you, but you can't keep teasing him ... he is a man. The next time the situation might be so compromising that y'all won't be able to stop things. You should also be worried about him easing his frustrations elsewhere. Know what I mean? Don't let that 'hoochie' get to you! Sex is obviously all she has going for her. I could tell that by the way she was dressed. I'm going back downstairs for a little while longer and then I'm coming back up to go to bed. Since the kids aren't here I can sleep as late as I want to tomorrow. You gonna' be all right?"

I shook my head yes.

As she walked out the door, she turned back around. "I apologize for coming down on you so hard. You know me."

I smiled as she closed the door.

Just as I was about to doze off there was another knock at the door. I never locked it after Kari left, so I didn't bother getting up to answer it.

"Come in."

Julian stuck his head in, "Are you awake?"

I looked at him and said, "Uh, huh."

He came in and sat on the bed, "Look Shelby, I need to understand something? I know we've already talked about this, but...are we or are we not going to make love? I'm only asking because I'm getting mixed messages from you. I need for you to help me understand one more time where we're at with this."

I sat up. "Nothing has changed. I still want to wait. I just think we both had a little too much to drink tonight and the mood and the moment just seemed right."

He kind of chuckled, "So you're saying the only reason that you were sitting on top of me unfastening my belt was because we were drunk? I don't know what's up with you, but I'm crazy in love with you girl and I want to make love ... to you!"

I wasn't sure what he was trying to say about me, but

I didn't think I liked it.

"Exactly what are you trying to say Julian?"

"Shelby, you know you want to make love to me just as much as I want to make love to you. You told me that tonight, but you're sitting here acting like the only reason that we were about to get busy was because you had a little too much to drink. What's up with that Shelby?"

I thought I was going to pop, but I stayed calm, "I never said I didn't want to have sex with you Julian ... because that's what it would be.... having sex. And you're right, I want to just as much as you do, maybe even more. It's just important to me to wait. I'm not some 'freak' like your girl Camilla. I want to make sure that we're going to be together, monogamously. This punanny is not free for the taking just because I care about you!"

Julian stood up. "I don't understand why you would think our relationship was anything other then monogamous. Baby, I'm not a boy. I haven't been a boy in a long time. We can't keep playing this game. We're 'not' going to keep playing this game! By the way, this has nothing to do with Camilla, this is about you and me."

He said what he had to say, turned and walked out of the room. While I was still sitting there trying to figure out where we were headed from there, Julian stuck his head back in the door.

"You need to lock this door until everybody's gone."

He locked the door and closed it behind him.

CHAPTER
14

$\mathscr{T}$he rest of the weekend was pretty humdrum. Saturday everybody slept late and when we got up Smokie and Julian fixed brunch. We spent the day looking at movies and sitting around the pool talking. We just kind of hung out with each other until Sunday morning. Kari and Sharrin's flight was leaving Sunday afternoon, so when we left that morning they bid their "farewells" to Julian and Smokie. As we rode to the airport later that afternoon Kari asked if everything was okay with Julian and me.

I looked at her and said, "Of course it is, why wouldn't it be?"

She looked at me and said, "I don't know! Y'all just didn't seem as lovey-dovey this morning."

I smiled and looked at Sharrin, "I think a more important question is what's up with Sharrin and Smokie?"

Sharrin laughed and told us that he was a really nice guy, but nothing was up. She said he was pretty deep! I just didn't see it, but then again Smokie and I had never sat down and had an intelligent conversation.

As I walked them to the gate Kari talked about how she couldn't live in Julian's world because she couldn't party like that more then once a year. Of course, Sharrin was just the opposite. She would party like that every weekend if she could. It was nice to know that they both had a good time.

Kari gave me a hug and said, "Take care of yourself!"

When Sharrin hugged me she said, "Thanks girl! You got yourself an awesome man. Take it slow!"

As their plane took off it was kind of sad to see them go because now it was back to reality. Julian was going to be going on tour again in a few weeks and there was a little tension between us. Maybe time and distance would do us some good.

October rolled around really fast and my relationship with Julian had been a little strained ever since the episode in his bedroom. We still talked every night and had dinner together as often as possible, but things were not quite the same. I figured it would blow over in a couple of more weeks. Time apart might be what we needed. He was going to be leaving for a two and a half month concert tour and he hadn't invited me to attend any of the concerts, but like I said, the time apart would probably do us some good. The saying goes "distance makes the heart grow fonder," but I knew that there was also another saying that says, "out of sight, out of mind!"

Julian and I had dinner at his house the night before he left for his tour. Dinner was good, but conversation was very light. I would like to believe that Julian had a lot on his mind. If Smokie hadn't shown up things may have gotten really uncomfortable. I have to give Smokie a lot of credit because he obviously sensed the mood when he walked into the room, so he didn't cut up like he usually did. At one point while they talked I cleared the table (we were eating in the kitchen) and loaded the dishwasher. Smokie was going on the tour with Julian, but of course he always traveled with Julian if he's going to be away for longer then a week. They were going over a list of things.

Smokie looked up at me and said, "Shelby, what shows will you need a pass for?"

I quickly turned around and looked at Smokie, then at Julian.

Before I could answer him Julian said, "I don't think Shelby is going to be able to make it this time man."

I looked at him and said, "Yea, Julian's right! The kids are going to be getting out for the holiday in a little over a month and then again in another month, so I need to be available. Maybe I'll be able to make it on the next tour."

Smokie looked at both of us and without missing a beat said, "I'll go ahead and save you two or three passes in the event you get a couple of free weekends."

At that moment I gained a newfound respect for Smokie. Without even saying a word he was telling us that we needed to make the time to be together while Julian was away.

Julian called me at work from the airport, right before he boarded his plane.

"Just wanted to hear your voice before I left. I also wanted to let you know that once I get all settled, and you know that could take a couple of days, I'll call you. I love you, all right?"

I kind of smiled and said, "Okay! I'm going to miss you! Don't forget to call me?"

He said, "Okay, gotta' go there're boarding the plane."

We said bye and I didn't hear from him again for a little over two weeks...

In a way I was kind of glad that Julian hadn't called, it gave me a lot of time to think. I hung out with Kyme and Tracie, we did a lot of talking and even spent a couple of weekends at Julian's house. I called Kari one night, just to hear the voice of reason. I really needed to hear someone say that things were going to be okay between Julian and me and who better then Kari.

"Hi Davis, is Kari home?"

Davis, Kari's husband, is not very talkative. He asked how I was doing and told me to hold on.

When she came to the phone her first question was, "What's wrong? Are you all right?"

I started laughing, "Of course I'm all right, nothing's wrong! Why would you ask me that?"

She calmed down and said, "Oh, okay then, what do you want?"

We both laughed! I just love my family's sick sense of humor.

"Look Kari, do you remember that weekend that you and Sharrin were here?"

She said, "Yea..."

I went on, "Well, things have been different between me and Julian every since then."

Kari asked, "What do you mean different?"

I almost felt silly talking to Kari about this.

"There's been like a silent tension between us. He and I haven't talked about it because we know why it's there. Do you think I'm going to lose him?"

Kari didn't say anything for a minute then she asked, "Shelby, do you really love Julian?"

I looked at the phone like that was the stupidest question I'd ever heard, "Of course I do..."

"Have you ever told him that you loved him?"

I thought about it. "No, I haven't..."

"Then how is he supposed to know it? We've already determined that you're not sixteen years old. Stop acting like this relationship stuff is brand new to you! You know you want to hear him tell you that he loves you. Don't you think he wants to hear that from you too? He's used to women throwing sex at him and calling it love. That you've gotten this beautiful man to agree to wait until you're married is wonderful, but you have to let him know that you love him Shell! You have to tell him. Know what I mean?"

I knew it was a good idea to call her. When I finally

heard from Julian his voice sounded like music to my ears.

"Hey baby it's me!"

I couldn't resist playing with him a little, so I said, "I can't stay on the line long, I'm expecting a call from my boyfriend any minute now."

He laughed, that was a good sign.

"So, how's the tour going? Any good groupie stories for me?"

He laughed again, "Nope! Things have been pretty sane. Shelby, I miss you girl! I want to apologize for the way I was acting before I left. There was no excuse for me to leave things with you like I did...and I'm sorry!"

I thought, "If I couldn't tell Julian that I loved him now, then I was crazy."

"I owe you and apology too. I know we should have talked about things before you left, but I don't know. I just didn't know what to say. So, I'm sorry too."

This man was going to be my husband and I knew it. We were soul mates, but I was still terrified to tell him that I loved him. He was talking, but I obviously was not paying attention.

"Shelby! What are you doing, watching TV? Did you hear what I just said?"

I had to apologize because I was off in my own little world for a minute there. "I'm sorry baby, my mind wandered for a minute. What did you say?"

"I was just saying that I loved you and I really want to see you."

How could I say no? "That is so sweet. That's why I love you."

"Excuse me, did you just say you loved me?"

It felt good, so I said it again, "Yea, I said I love you boo. I love you!"

There was silence, so I had to ask if he was still on the phone...and he was.

"Yea, uhm...man! Look, let me know if you can fly here this weekend. If you can't that's okay, we'll do something special when I get back!"

I said, "Okay..."

Okay, so I did it. I told Julian that I loved him. For me this meant we had taken our relationship to the next level.

I told Tracie and Kyme about my conversation with Julian. Both of them were not surprised by Julian's response, but they were glad that I finally told the man that I loved him. Kyme even wanted to know what I expected after a whole year.

"How much longer do you think you could have gone without telling him that you loved him?"

Tracie was funny because she said, "Girl, stop acting like you don't know...you're scaring me!"

Pretty funny friends, huh? I didn't tell them about the surprise that I was going to have waiting at Julian's house when he got back. I had Smokie's pager number, so I decided to page him and find out exactly when they were coming back. Of course I had a key and the security code to Julian's house, so it wouldn't be a problem getting in. I came to the conclusion that Julian and I were going to be married and now that he "knew" that I loved him we could go ahead and make love. How much more special could I make his return home? It was going to be nice waking up in his arms after spending the night with him.

Smokie eventually returned my 911 pages ... three days later. He said he was busy, so many groupies, so little time. I don't know why I expected anything different. I guess he turns the real charm on and off like a light switch. Before he would tell me when they were coming back he wanted to know if I would call Sharrin and have her waiting for him when he got back. I told him he was sick! Just when I thought I was going to have to give up on him he started talking like a human being.

"Look Shelby, all jokes aside. I'm glad you and my boy handled your business. He ain't right without you. You got to be the one! I know it's hard to take me seriously most of the time, but Ju'man is like my brother. Don't hurt my boy, all right?"

His display of emotions for Julian and the sincerity in his voice took me by surprise.

"All right Smokie, you have my word."

I was feeling especially warm and fuzzy, so I told Smokie that if he wanted me to I would call Sharrin and tell her that he had a round-trip ticket at the airport for her, her own suite at their hotel, and a backstage pass to the next weekend concert. He was most appreciative and he told me he would take "good" care of my people. He eventually got around to telling me that they would be back on December 23rd. The timing was pretty good because school would be out, so I didn't have to worry about leaving Julian's house early the next morning or asking for the day off.   It was hard to believe that we were finally going to do this thing!

It was hard to keep my plans secret from Julian because I knew this was a pivotal point for us. It was hard to keep it from Tracie and Kyme too, especially with them continually asking me what I was going to do for Julian when he got back. Even Sharrin wanted to know if I was planning a party for him. The concert was getting very good reviews in every city that it went to, so everybody was expecting me to throw a welcome home party for Julian. I didn't want to have a lot of people around when he got back. I wanted to spend some quiet time with him. The weeks before he left were terrible for both of us, so I really didn't want to share him with anybody as soon as he got back.

I reasoned that I'd wait a week and then Smokie and I could put our heads together and throw a little something together, but not before then.

Smokie gave me a general idea when Julian would get back.   I expected him to come in on a late flight on December 23rd, so my plan was to pickup lots of scented candles, a bottle of Cristal, and some fruit; grapes, kiwi, and strawberries (to munch on afterwards...).   I could go through Julian's CD collection to find a nice jazz CD. Oh yea, I also had to go by Victoria's Secret to get something sexy. "It's all in the presentation you know." I actually had to laugh at myself when I had that thought! I asked Smokie to make sure Julian came straight home.

I thought maybe I would also go by a florist and get some flower petals to throw on the bed. Okay, everything was all ready! I had dinner with Kyme and Tracie and we spent most of the time talking about Julian and about the party they thought I should have for him (because they felt like a party). I promised them that Smokie and I would get together and plan a party for the following weekend.

At one point, during dinner Tracie asked, "What's wrong with you, your mind has been somewhere else all night?"

I smiled and said, "My man is coming home tonight and I haven't seen him in weeks. Can't I be a little excited about that?"

Kyme laughed and said, "She wouldn't know, she doesn't have a man!"

We all laughed!

Tracie response was "That's okay, Y'all can laugh at me now, but when I do get a man I don't want y'all to be mad when I don't have time for y'all!"

I was absolutely beside myself. I was ready for dinner to end, so that I could get everything set up at Julian's house. By the time we finished dinner, cleaned up, and talked a little while, it was a little after 9:00pm. That was actually good timing because it would give me time to run home and pick up my suitcase that I had packed earlier in the day. I would get to Julian's around 10:00pm, set up everything, put the Cristal on ice, and take a shower by 11:00pm and Julian should walk through the back door sometime between midnight and 1:00am. Yep, I had it all planned out. When I arrived at Julian's house I was so nervous that I couldn't remember the code for the security gate, so I parked up front. I put my suitcase next to the stairwell after I let myself in. I headed for the kitchen to prepare a little fruit tray and to get an ice bucket for the Cristal. It took me about ten or fifteen minutes to find what I was looking for. Once I set the tray up I put it in the refrigerator and I put the Cristal on ice. I went back to the foyer and grabbed my suitcase. I headed for Julian's bedroom thinking, "I can't believe that this is finally going to happen!" The timing was right and I was absolutely positive that this would be the last thing that Julian would expect. As I approached Julian's room I noticed that the door was slightly ajar and I thought, "that's weird, why is his bedroom door closed, none of the others are?" I slowly opened the door and the only thing that I could see was the big behind of a woman, in her underwear, on all fours, straddling someone on the bed! I could see a man's hands on the woman's waist and they looked like Julian's, but I thought, "Impossible, Julian's not back yet!" As I was thinking this to myself, I heard the woman say, "Julian, just relax, let me do this. It'll be like old times." I went into shock! I couldn't say anything! I pulled the door closed and just stood there. I wanted to run, but my feet wouldn't move! I wanted to scream, but I couldn't make a sound! I slowly backed away from the door. The walk from the bedroom door to the staircase had never before taken as long as it did that night. It felt like the longest walk I had ever taken in my life. Once I reached the stairs I turned and looked back one more time, thinking that perhaps my eyes and ears had deceived me, and wondering how this could have happened?

When I finally reached my car I got in and just sat there. I don't remember for how long. I felt sick to my stomach, but I couldn't cry. I didn't look back as I drove away. I couldn't believe that Julian would do this to me! I had been such a fool! I was about to give this man the most precious thing I had...and he was having sex with someone else? I felt like such a fool! I couldn't go home because he would eventually call me there, so I decided to call Kyme and ask her if I could come back over there. I pulled off the highway to call her and to throw up. I was embarrassed because it was late (by now it was about midnight), but I didn't want to go home.

"Kyme, this is Shelby..."

Kyme wasn't completely awake yet, but she could sense, by my voice, that something wrong.

"Shelby, what are you doing calling so late? Are you all right?"

I didn't want to tell her what had just happened, but I had to tell her something.

"Look, things didn't go down like I had planned tonight, but I don't want to talk about it right now. I need somewhere to stay for a few days."

Kyme, being the friend that she is said, "Yea, of course! Come on over."

I made it to Kyme's duplex in one piece. I couldn't remember anything about the ride from Julian's house to Kyme's. It was like I had driven with my eyes closed. I sat in front of Kyme's place for a few minutes to gather my thoughts and to regain some semblance of composure. I was actually physically and mentally drained by all that had transpired. I took a deep breath as I grabbed my suitcase and headed for the door. I felt silly for even being out in the streets so late. I felt out of pocket, lost. I really didn't know what to do next. It was kind of silly, but I didn't know where I belonged. When Kyme opened the door she was wide-awake.

She stood to the side as I walked in, "Come on in, unless you want to stand out there a little longer."

I looked at her and gave her a half smile because I didn't feel like responding.

Kyme closed the door and said, "Okay...do you want to tell me what's going on? Is Julian all right?"

I shook my head and told her that I really just wanted to go to bed.

I don't think I ever slept that night. I just lay there thinking about what I saw. Kyme knocked on the bedroom door around 7:30am (for both of us that's late) and I told her to come on in. She said good morning and sat on the bed.

"You look terrible. Did you even sleep last night?"

I kind of laughed, "Thanks and good morning to you

too!"

She smiled, "But seriously, are you okay? What happened last night?"

I looked at her and tears welled up in my eyes, "Kyme, I'm just not ready to talk about it yet..."

She shook her head, "Okay, you know I'm here for you when you're ready!"

I smiled, "I know. Thank you."

She gave me a hug and asked if I wanted something for breakfast.

Kyme doesn't cook, so I was amazed that she offered to fix breakfast for me. "I must look pretty darn bad for you to offer to cook breakfast for me?"

Kyme stood up and put her hand on her hips, "Girl, I'm offering to pick you something up from McDonald's. You don't look that bad!"

That evening we caught up with Tracie and we went to the beach, not to swim, just to walk around and talk. In the evening when the sun is setting and the wind is blowing the beach is the best place in the world to be. It's very relaxing to take a slow walk or to lay out on a lounge chair, wrapped up in a blanket, and listen to the waves come in. You forget about everything. Of course, being at the beach made me think about the first time Julian took me there. I smiled as I remembered how he drove me out there for a romantic evening, after ignoring everything I had previously told him about not wanting to get involved in a relationship with him. How could he fool me? Why didn't I see it?

I'm not "that" green. I felt a tear roll down my cheek. Tracie must have seen it because she asked if I was okay.

I looked over at her and said, "No, but I will be!"

We stayed at the beach for a couple of hours and then we headed home. I decided that evening that I'd take a trip home to spend some time with my family. That would help me get my head straight. When we got back to Kyme's house I excused myself and took a shower and went to bed.

CHAPTER
15

I finally checked my messages late Sunday afternoon, but only after Kyme asked me if I had talked with Julian. I was kind of hesitant about checking them because I knew that Julian had probably called and left me several messages. Just as I had expected, I had 18 messages and they were all from him! I received ten on Saturday, and so far on Sunday I had received eight more. The last message said that he was really worried about me, that he thought maybe I had gone out of town, but he wasn't sure and he didn't want to call my family and worry them, in case I wasn't there. He also said he hadn't slept all night. I bet! After listening to my messages all I could do was close my eyes and shake my head. Kyme must have been watching me.

"Girl, you all right? Is Julian back in town? What?"

I looked at her and said, "Yea...he's back. I, uhm, won't be seeing him any more though."

Kyme looked at me, "What do you mean you won't be seeing him any more? Didn't y'all make up?"

I started crying. "He's been seeing somebody else!"

Kyme stopped what she was doing and said, "What?" She walked over to me and grabbed my arm. "Shelby, I don't understand? Why would you think something like that?"

I began to sob uncontrollably, "I caught him having sex with her! I saw him with my own eyes ... in his bed!"

I glanced up at her and she had tears in her eyes too, "Shelby, I'm so sorry...are you sure though? Maybe it was Smokie. You know how Julian is about letting other people use his house when he's not there?"

I closed my eyes and said, "It was that same girl, Camilla. I heard her voice and I saw her naked butt in bed with Julian!"

Kyme asked me very quietly, in almost a whisper, "What are you gonna do?"

I looked down at my hands and said, "I don't know. I just don't know! Well, yea I do! I'm just not going to see him any more. I don't want to talk with him or see him. I told this man I loved him. Kyme, I feel like such a fool! Like I was some kind of challenge...a game. He was only trying to wait me out, hoping that I would have sex with him and then he could put another notch on his belt. Ole' smooth Jules Brishard almost got me too!"

Kyme looked at me baffled, "What do you mean?"

I smiled at her, "Oh yea I forgot, you didn't know, but I had a grand surprise all lined up for Mr. Brishard when he got back. I bought a couple of outfits from Victoria's Secret. I even went into my savings and sprung for a bottle of Cristal. Would you believe that I even bought candles and flower petals for the bedroom and fruit to snack on afterwards? Girl, I had it all planned. I was going to stay with him for the entire weekend. I guess this is what I get for compromising my integrity for a man. I wanted to wait, but I figured we could go ahead and have sex. What would it hurt? We love each other and I knew we were going to get married! I guess it's better that I found out about things now, rather then later." I put my hand over my mouth and squinted my eyes as I looked at Kyme, "I saw them in bed together! I opened the door and I saw this naked woman on top of Julian and he had his hands all over her. Humph!"

Kyme sat there and looked at me, slowly shaking her head from side to side. She never said another word.

To completely avoid seeing or talking with Julian, I decided to go visit my family as planned. I knew I would feel safe and secure at home with my mom and dad. The only problem I foresaw was Coco. He talked to Julian pretty regularly and I didn't want him to tell Julian that I was there. I would just have to tell Coco what happened, well, at least some of what happened anyway.

When I pulled into the drive, I felt as though a great weight had been lifted off of my shoulders. I got out of the car to open the gate, hoping the dogs didn't attack me. My mom and dad have two dogs, two cats, four birds, and a bunch of fish. They both love animals, so going home was like a trip to the zoo. I hadn't told anybody I was coming, so nobody was expecting me. When I pulled up to the garage, I blew my horn a couple of times. My mom hated that, so I knew she would be the first one to look outside. As soon as she saw me she raced to the car and greeted me with a big ole momma hug.

"I didn't know you were coming home baby!"

I told my mom that I hadn't planned on being there, but things changed so I thought I'd come home for a while.

My mom hugged me again, "I'm glad your plans changed. How long are you going to be here?" I smiled and said, "The whole week."

I unpacked my suitcase and sat on the bed for a minute. I looked around my room and tried to remember how it used to feel as a teenager when I had a problem and I sat in my room. I remembered how me and my sisters would get together in there when we were younger and talk about everything; school, teachers, clothes, boys, love, what our husbands were going to be like, and how many children we were going to have. Those were the days! We all had pretty unrealistic expectations. Well, I guess Kari's expectations weren't so unrealistic. Her plan was always to first go to college and get her Masters in Elementary education. Afterwards she was going to meet her husband in college or soon after and date him for three or four years. Then she was going to work a few years. She was going to marry by the age of 29 or 30, have two children by the time she was 40, and then be a stay at home mom. I guess being the oldest child made her more organized and more in tune with everything. I don't really know if that's the reason Kari's life is right on the money.

Sharrin, on the other hand, has always been totally impractical and has always wanted to live a very opulent lifestyle. She dated the best looking guy in high school (they were also Senior Superlatives, Cutest Couple and Sharrin was also Best Dressed). When she went to college she dated the finest and possibly the wealthiest guy on campus. Her plan was plain and simple, she was going to marry rich. Of course, she went to college so that she could get a job to support her spending habits, but after college her ideas about life and marriage changed. Now she doesn't care about getting married because she makes big bucks as a PR person. She dates and figures she might consider marriage when she turns 40 yrs old or so.

Then there was me. I thought...before I could finish my thought my mom walked in.

"You all right baby? You look kind of funny."

I smiled at her and said, "I'm fine mom."

She sat down on the bed next to me and put her hand on top of mine, "I mean, are you all right?"

I said it again, "I'm fine."

This time my mom smiled and said, "Julian called last night. Coleman wasn't here, so he talked with me for a little while. Said he hadn't talked with you since he's been back. He's worried about you, but he didn't want to worry us. He thought maybe you told him your plans, but he forgot them. So, I'm going to ask you one more time. Are you all right?"

I grinned at her and sighed, "No, not really, but I'll be okay."

My mom squeezed my hand and said, "I'm not going to ask you what's going on, but if you want to talk I'll be glad to listen."

As she stood up she said, "There is one thing I'm going to say. He's not perfect, but neither are you! Think about it."

My mom walked out of the room, but her wisdom lingered behind. I do love Julian, but how could I forgive infidelity. Better yet, how could I forget it? My mom came from a different school of thought. I think women her age tolerated a lot more then women my age. I didn't want to be married to someone I had to tolerate. I wanted to be married to someone that I could love.

When Coco got home he hugged me and asked about Julian. It kind of pissed me off that he was so fascinated with my boyfriend.

I smiled at him and said, "I'm fine, my trip was fine, and I'll be here for about a week. How's Coco doing?"

He laughed and said, "What are you tripping about? Did Julian tell you that I was going to be up there for New Years Eve?"

I sarcastically answered, "No he didn't. He doesn't tell me everything."

Coco still wasn't getting it because he thought that maybe we could fly back together. I had to deflate his plans because I wasn't going back until the weekend after New

Years.

When my daddy got home he kissed me on my forehead and asked how I was doing, as he walked through the room to go take a shower. When he came back to get his dinner he stood in front of me.

"So, what's going on with you and the singer guy? Your mom told me he called last night. Y'all had a fight?"

My daddy is a very sweet and intelligent man who lacks any form of tact. He says what he's thinking and asks very direct questions. I followed my dad into the kitchen.

"No, we haven't had a fight. Why would you even ask that?"

My daddy turned around and looked at me and said, "Because you're here...without him."

Well, my first night home was exactly what I expected, chit-chat and questions. I called Sharrin and Kari to make arrangements to spend one night with each one of them. My trip home just wouldn't be right if I didn't spend some time with my sisters. Even though we talked often, I still missed spending time with my sisters and doing "sister stuff." My second day in town my mom and I spent the day out and about because she felt the need to dedicate a whole day to gracing me with her years of wisdom. My mom thinks the world of Julian, even though she hadn't officially met him yet, and she really wanted me to give him a chance. She didn't want to know what he did because she says it's irrelevant. She says part of loving someone is overlooking his or her faults and helping them work on overcoming them. My mom assures me that all of her children have faults and she expects the people that love them to work with them because it's not her job to do that anymore. My mother is great! She raised us to be thinkers and for the most part we all are. I guess I should spend more time thinking about a resolution to my problem and not the problem itself.

My first night out I spent at Sharrin's and I must say her apartment is the ultimate chick place, very art deco, and she has the ultimate view of the ocean. We sat up most of the night talking after we came back from dinner (we went out for dinner because Sharrin doesn't cook). It seemed like Sharrin had been thinking about Smokie a lot. While we were talking she kept referring to "Omar." At first I was thinking that it was a new beau, but a couple of times she said something about "the concert." I was tired of trying to figure it out, so I finally asked.

"Who is Omar? He must have really put the whammy on you!"

Sharrin looked at me kind of puzzled. "I'm talking about Smokie."

I started laughing. "Smokie is an Omar? I would never have guessed! He looks more like a Chris or an Antoine. Omar!"

I guess I must have insulted him or her or whatever because Sharrin said, "What do you mean by that?"

I smiled and asked, "Mean by what? I didn't say anything."

Sharrin looked at me and said, "I bet you've never even sat down and talked with Omar. He's a really, really nice guy. Obviously he's a little complicated because he's nothing like he appears to be. He's probably just as sweet as Julian is. They're a lot a like you know! That's why they're so close."

I wondered what happened when she went to Julian's concert? It was apparent that Smokie showed her a really good time. He must have really wined and dined her. He had made a very good impression on Sharrin. I don't even think it's possible for a man to fool Sharrin. I've always considered her to be an excellent judge of character and plus she only goes for guys with lots of money and lots of personality. If they have a major character flaw she has them out of the picture so fast they don't know what happened, and even then they remain her friends. I'm glad that she's spent some quality time with Smokie. I still haven't figured him out, but if she had, good for her.

I must have been lost in thought because as Sharrin was leaving the room I thought I heard her say that Smokie had told her what was going on between Julian and me. When she came back into the room I asked her what she said.

"What were you saying when you walked out the room? I thought you said something about me and Julian?"

As she sat down she said, "I did...I said, Omar told me that something bad was going on between you and Julian. He's not sure what it is, but he knows that y'all haven't seen each other since Julian has been back in town. So, what's up with that?"

I looked at her kind of smugly because I didn't really want to tell her what happened because she and "Omar" seemed to be pretty buddy, buddy. She might tell him...and of course he would go right back and tell Julian. Instead I told Sharrin that I finally realized that Julian's lifestyle wasn't really the kind of lifestyle that I wanted to be a part of. I just wasn't sure how to tell Julian how I felt.

As I watched her, she looked convinced that I was telling the truth. Good for me because I wasn't in the mood to hear a lecture about Julian's virtues.

Around mid-morning the next day I left for my other sister's house. I hung out at Kari's doing kid stuff all day, including lunch and museums. When Davis got home he didn't talk very much. He ate his dinner, played with the kids, sat and talked with me for a few minutes, and then went to bed. Kari and I sat up until about midnight talking about my ex-husband. Kari, along with everyone else, was still shocked by the fact that Lorenz appeared to have his stuff together, but was really a closet alcoholic and a philanderer. I asked Kari how often she thought people lived that kind of dual life? She seemed to think it was the exception and not the rule. If that was the case, how was it that I met two men in a row that did it? It felt so nice to spend time with Kari that I didn't want to taint it by talking about my current situation with Julian. I never mentioned finding Julian in bed with Camilla. I knew Kari would give me some good insight and a lot to think about, but I thought I should work this one out on my own.

When I got back to my mom and dad's place I found out that Coco had talked with Julian and told him that I was there, so I had a message to call him as soon as possible. I thought, "Great, now I have to talk to him!" I didn't know if I was ready, so I decided to call him about an hour and a half before my flight, that way I could use my flight as an excuse to get off of the phone. As I'm hanging up the phone I could make plans for dinner...to break things off. I thought that was a good idea. I wouldn't have time to explain anything because of my flight and I could go home and sit down and gather my thoughts before meeting him for dinner. I didn't get a chance to fuss at Coco because he had already left for the New Year's Eve party that Julian was either having or going to. I spent the last couple of days at home hanging out, talking with my mom and fishing with my dad. Both of them kept reminding me to call my boyfriend.

The Friday before I left Sharrin, Kari and the kids, and Kristoff, his wife, and his kids came over to have dinner and spend the night. We stayed up all night talking and playing cards. It was just like what we used to do when we were kids, except Collin was out of town on business so he wasn't there with us. I got up early the next morning because I couldn't sleep. My mom fixed breakfast, so I had breakfast with her and dad (they were the only ones up). My mom told me not to worry about things so much and my dad told me to be careful and think before I act. It was almost like they knew what I was getting ready to do. I assured them that I wouldn't do anything crazy. I didn't want them to worry about me. I was the only one of their children that didn't live in the same state or for that matter in a 45-mile radius of them, so they very seldom knew what was going on with me. I knew they worried about me, but at the same time they also knew that I could take care of myself. My dad's solution to worrying about me being so far away was to just get me married again. I knew that he was hoping it would be Julian because, like everybody else, he was very fond of him too, and he hadn't even officially met him either. Didn't look like that was going to happen though and that would be okay. I could think of worse things than not being Julian's wife.

As I got ready to leave for the airport I called Julian. He answered on the first ring.

"Hello..."

I paused before I said anything, "Hi Julian, this is Shelby. Sorry for not calling before now."

He was obviously glad to hear from me.

"Girl I thought you had disappeared off the face of the earth for a few days there. I apologize for calling your parents, but I got kind of worried. I know crazy things happen and I just wanted to make sure that nothing had happened to my baby!"

I assured him that I was okay. I told him I couldn't talk long because I was on my way to the airport, but I could meet him for dinner at Houston's downtown on Main street around 6:30pm after I arrived. He agreed to meet me, so we hung up and I left for the airport. As I put the receiver on the hook I had a thought. I remembered once telling Julian that I believed we could work out any problems that we would have. I guess I really didn't mean that. I absolutely dreaded leaving my family and going back to real life. Fortunately school would be starting Monday, so work would keep me occupied.

My flight landed on time, so I went straight home and took a nap. When I woke up I still had several hours before dinner, so I looked over some files that I had brought home from work. I couldn't concentrate, so I watched a little TV. I got dressed at about 5:45pm and left for the restaurant. My intention was to get there early and have a drink (or two) to calm my nerves. I had been having anxiety attacks all day. I couldn't believe that it was going to end like this. How could I be so wrong about Julian? He seemed nice enough. Not perfect, but good. Was it possible that I was wrong and maybe it was somebody else in the bed? Maybe that Camilla knew I was coming and she set it up to look like she and Julian were having sex? But how would she know that I was going to be there?" Okay, I was losing it! I was beginning to unravel. I was thinking like a crazy woman. I guess I was grasping for straws.

I saw Julian before he saw me. One thing sure hadn't changed, "The boy looked good!" As he approached the table he flashed one of his million dollar smiles. I managed to return a closed lip smile. He walked straight toward me and attempted to kiss me on the lips. Without even thinking about it, I turned my head and he kissed my cheek. I know he was surprised because he stepped back and looked at me sort of puzzled.

As he sat down he said, "So, what's going on Shelby? Where have you been for the last couple of weeks? I've been leaving messages for you all over town. I went by your condo and I even went by the school a few times, knowing it was closed."

I took a deep breath as I sipped on my glass of wine. I didn't look at him as I started to speak, I couldn't.

"I've been doing a lot of thinking the last couple of weeks and I think, uhm, I think we need to slow things down...with us."

As I ran my finger around the rim of my glass I looked up at Julian.

"Maybe even consider seeing other people."

Julian sat back in his chair and kind of squinted his eyes as he looked at me.

"Where is all of this coming from?"

I could barely stand to look at him, partially because it still hurt to think about him with another woman and partially because I loved him so much.

"I know that this relationship has been hard for you Julian...because you haven't been able to have sex..."

Julian stopped me.

"This isn't about me, I can speak for myself! What's

up? I mean, what's going on Shelby? Look baby..." (and he leaned closer to me). I don't know what's wrong, but we can fix it! You gotta' talk to me though. You're coming out of left field with this. How long have you felt this way? Is it Smokie? What?"

I just wanted to get up and walk out. I wasn't going to lie to him and I couldn't believe he was sitting there acting like he didn't know what was going on. You know, I guess he didn't know. I saw him, he didn't see me. So, as far as he was concerned I don't know that he's been with someone else. I wondered if he'd been with any other women or if he just split his time between the two of us?

I took a deep breath and said, "Look, let's just do this. You may not believe it right now, but it's the best thing...for both of us!"

I had never seen Julian look so hurt.

"Shelby, I can't read your mind, so I don't know what's going on right now. I'm kind of confused because I thought we loved each other? If you've found somebody else, that's cool, but that's what you need to tell me. I'm not gonna lie to you, I'm hurting right now. I feel like you just snatched my heart out and kicked it across the room...for no apparent reason. When I first met you, you told me you didn't like to play games. But right now I'm feeling played! I feel even more foolish because I want to beg you not to do this, but I'm not going to beg. Let me say this though, if I've done or said anything out of pocket, to hurt you, then just tell me 'cause we can fix that. I can make that right. I love you

Shelby, you know that! I know you love me too, so I don't understand what's going on?"

As he stood up he said, "Just like that, huh? You say it's over and it's just over, no explanation, nothing? You say it's the "best thing" for both of us and I'm supposed to take it like a man I guess? What about the last few months Shelby, didn't they mean anything to you? If they didn't then you're a great actress, but I don't believe that." Julian walked around the table, grabbed me by my shoulders and lifted me to my feet. He kissed me right there in front of everybody! When I opened my eyes he was standing there looking at me.

All he said before he turned and walked away was, "Tell me 'that' wasn't right!"

I just stood there and watched him as he walked out of my life.

CHAPTER
16

*S*chool started, so work definitely kept my mind occupied during the day. I couldn't concentrate very well, but it kept me busy. Sometimes I would have to go to the rest room to put a little cold water on my face because of a brief crying spell. The nights were harder though because when I was home alone or when Tracie and Kyme were busy, it was hard not to pick up the phone and call Julian. I was determined not to do it though. I couldn't do it! I'd lay in bed thinking about the day that we met a thousand times. I always thought about the day at the beach, working out with him at his house, the times we almost made love, the time I told him I loved him. Sometimes I would laugh out loud or smile because most of the time we spent together was good...happy. Actually, all of our time together was good. I didn't know what to think about that. Even our arguments were pleasant. I still questioned why Julian would tell me he could wait, but then turn around and have sex with someone else? I was having a harder time with breaking up with Julian then I did with divorcing my ex-husband. What was up with that? I had never cried so much in my life. I had to take a couple of vacation days at the end of the month to recuperate.

February came and it seemed like my stream of tears had dried up, just a little. Julian was going to be on the music awards, Kyme and Tracie made sure I knew it. They invited themselves over to watch it at my house.

"...and the award for Best New Soul/R&B Artist goes to...Jules Brishard for his CD, Subtle Lover." Kyme and Tracie clapped and screamed for Julian, but I didn't. I sat there and looked at him. It had been a little over two months since the last time I saw him and he still looked good, real good. I smiled to myself. Pictures of Julian with his freak immediately crowded out my thoughts.

My smile gave way to tears and I begin to feel sick to my stomach, so I got up to go into the kitchen. Kyme grabbed me by my hand and asked, "You okay?"

I could have easily lied and said, "Yea, I'm fine", but I didn't. I told the truth.

"No, I'm not all right, so I'm going to step out of the room for just a minute to get myself a glass of water and some fresh air."

In the background I could hear Julian thanking people. I heard him thanking his mom and grandma for all of their love and support. As I left the room Kyme looked up at me with puppy dog eyes and asked me to stay until Julian was finished. Suddenly Tracie hollered out.

"Y'all listen, listen!"

Julian was still on stage thanking people, or so I

thought...

"None of this means anything if you don't have someone to share it with, so I'd like to dedicate this award to
someone who means everything to me. I'd gladly give up all
of this to have her back in my life. Shell, I love you!"

Tracie and Kyme turned and looked at me.

Tracie said, "Ooh Shell girl, he's talking about you."

I knew he was and I was very moved, but I wasn't
going to cry in front of Tracie and Kyme. I was tired of crying in front of them.

Later during the awards show Julian performed. When
the host, Chris Rock, introduced him he said it was a new
song, "Feel Me?" that would be on his next CD. I sat down
to listen to it.

I thought about you a lot today, couldn't get you off
my mind
It seems like forever since I've seen you
When I lay down, put my head on the pillow, you were
right there
Felt your breath on my cheek
I knew it was you because pictures of you went
through my mind, and it felt good
It felt like you
Do you feel me when I see you in my dreams?
Did you feel me when our tongues touched?
What about when I held you in my arms?
Did you feel me when I looked at you and drank up
your love?

Do you feel me?

When I'm laughing with my friends I smile because I'm
thinking 'bout you
How you used to walk up behind me and put your
arms around me
How you danced when you walked
How you held me with the sparkle in your eyes
How your perfume demanded my attention...
and made me feel you

Do you feel me when I see you in my dreams?
Did you feel me when our tongues touched?
What about when I held you in my arms?
Did you feel me when I looked at you and drank up
your love?
Do you feel me?

It's no accident that I feel you
You let me in your love
And you captured my soul with your passion
So why can't you feel me?
I feel you, I feel you, and I feel you

Do you feel me when I see you in my dreams?
Did you feel me when our tongues touched?
What about when I held you in my arms?
Did you feel me when I looked at you and drank up

your love?
Do you feel me? Why can't you feel me?

Kyme looked over at me and said, "You know he's talking about you. Girl, call that man and at least get his version of what happened."

As Kyme and Tracie were leaving they both gave me a hug.

Kyme whispered in my ear, "He loves you Shelby, at least talk to him. I don't think he'd ever do anything to hurt you. He's not Lorenz. I'll call you tomorrow."

I looked at her and gave her a half smile. I appreciated and understood what she was saying, but that wasn't enough to make things better. It was hard to get to sleep that night. I couldn't stop thinking about Julian or his song. He looked so good! The more I thought about him the more I realized how sad he looked. He looked like he'd lost a little weight too. He was wrong about one thing, I could definitely feel him.

I know what I saw that night and no one could convince me otherwise. Lorenz used to play head games like that with me all of the time. I'd get a hang up call, so I'd *69 it and the woman on the other end would say, "No one called from this number." I wouldn't even argue with her, I would just ask Lorenz to stop his friends from calling the house and hanging up. He would always get mad at me for calling them back. He would tell me that I was making things up and that I was paranoid.

When I found cards and pictures he'd say, "They're just friends, stop tripping! You're always trying to make something out of nothing." I can still hear him, "Stop trying to make something out of nothing..."

Lorenz was sleeping with so many women I couldn't keep count and now Julian's playing the same game, except I caught him in bed with a woman. And what do my friends say to me? The same thing that Lorenz used to say, "You're making something out of nothing."

About three weeks after the awards show I had a message on my machine from Smokie. Because I wasn't home he said he would call me back later that night. "Oh boy, Smokie was going to call me back." It was strange, but I actually kind of missed talking with him. I knew he was going to call back and talk about Julian, but I figured we could use the time to talk about Sharrin too. I took off my workout clothes and took a shower and fixed something to eat. While I ate I read over some information that I had brought home with me. It was getting kind of late, so I went and got in the bed. "I guess Smokie decided not to call after all." I looked at the clock on my nightstand one last time before I turned off the lights. It was 11:00pm and I couldn't wait up anymore for Smokie.

Of course, as soon as I closed my eyes the phone rang...it was Smokie.

"Uhhh, hello."

"Hey Shelby, this is Smokie. Sorry for calling so late, I just got off of the phone with Sharrin."

I smiled, "Oh, hey Omar."

Smokie laughed, "Okay, I ain't mad at 'cha or your people because I know who told you my name. Look here though, you know why I called, it's about my man Julian. We've known each other since we were little fellas and I know him as well as I know myself. My boy is hurtin' real bad right now. He says everything is all-good, but it's not. He told me how you felt about me, so I want to apologize to you because I didn't mean any harm. It's just my way of weedin' the chickenheads out. Julian has been all about you since day one, so I didn't want to see him get burnt. Know what I mean? There are a lot of women out there who'll put on a good game face to be with my boy, but they ain't really 'bout nothing! They just want to be with "Jules Brishard." Know what I mean? They just want the name, the glamour, and the money that goes along with it. So as his brother, it's my job to watch his back!"

I sat up in the bed to listen more closely.

He continued, "I hate breakin' down and calling you, but it's either this or dealing with my man like he is. I can't keep watching him like this. It's a trip! He don't wanna eat. He's having a hard time sleepin'. He can't concentrate...you know what I'm talkin' about. If I have anything to do with you staying away then be mad at me, take it out on me, don't take it out on Julian."

He stopped talking, so I took that as my cue to say something.

"Smokie, please don't think that this whole thing is

about you. Since you've been talking to my sister I've really come to realize that you aren't so bad after all...I hope! Really, this is bigger then, uhm, how I've felt about you in the past. This is about Julian and me. How I feel about his lifestyle, how I feel about maintaining my own identity..."

Smokie interrupted long enough to say, "I don't understand what you're saying, explain."

I took a deep breath, "I don't want to give up myself...what I believe is right and wrong just to be with him. I mean, I don't want to find myself accepting stuff, things that I don't think are acceptable in a relationship...just because I want to be with him. I've never been one to settle."

Smokie stopped me again, "Okay...you know that Julian is getting large and he has a bunch of groupies following him everywhere, but it's part of my job to keep them away from him, as much as possible. You know he has his head on straight and he isn't tryin' to get with none of them! My boy ain't that green and I don't think he would ask you for anything that he can't give back."

I couldn't believe that Smokie and I were having a civilized conversation...about my relationship with Julian, his best friend, no less. It would be good to get his perspective on things, but at the same time, how could I really expect him to tell me the truth? He's looking out for Julian's best interest, not mine! It's difficult to think rationally when you're emotional. I really didn't mind talking with Smokie, but before I said another word I had to ask him a question.

"Smokie tell me one thing. Would you lie for Julian?"

He laughed out loud and said, "Of course I would if I had to, but I wouldn't lie to you!"

That was not exactly what I was expecting to hear. Actually, I thought he would say no.

I grinned and shook my head, "Smokie..."

I guess I paused too long, "Shelby, you still there? What's wrong?"

I thought I could get through this conversation without getting overly emotional.

"Smokie, I really love Julian...I do and I'm terrified! I don't want to be hurt again. It's too much! I want to trust him, but it's hard with women always wanting to...trying to be with him, and what about his ex-girlfriends? I don't want to compete for his love."

Smoke stopped me, "Whoa, I can personally assure you that there is no competition. My boy loves you! As far as women go, it's only a couple that can truthfully say that they were his ladies. The few others that he's gone out with were just for the night or the event...and I don't mean that in a bad way! Julian isn't like other brothers, he treats women good, sometimes too good I think! So, you don't have to worry 'bout Julian messing 'round on ya'. Matter of fact, Julian has been played a time or two himself."

I thought Smokie said he wouldn't lie to me, but he was on the phone doing just that! Julian was with another woman and I know it because I saw it with my own two eyes and for Smokie to have the audacity to sit on the phone and tell me that Julian "would not" cheat on me made me so mad that I could scream! I don't know what came over me.

" HOW CAN YOU IN ONE BREATH TELL ME YOU WOULDN'T LIE TO ME AND IN THE NEXT BREATH DO JUST THAT? YOU KNOW, AS WELL AS I DO, THAT Y'ALL ARE SO CLOSE THAT YOU WOULD LIE FOR HIM! YOU'LL LIE TO ANYBODY, INCLUDING ME, IF YOU FELT LIKE YOU HAD TO! LET ME TELL YOU SOME-THING YOU MIGHT NOT KNOW. WHEN JULIAN CAME BACK OFF THE ROAD, FROM HIS LAST TOUR, I WANTED TO SUPRISE HIM. I WANTED TO DO SOME-THING REALLY SPECIAL FOR YOUR FRIEND, YOUR BROTHER. DO YOU REMEMBER ME CALLING YOU AND ASKING YOU ABOUT SPECIFIC TIMES AND DATES? I WANTED TO BE AT HIS HOUSE WHEN HE GOT BACK IN TOWN. I WANTED THE NIGHT TO BE REALLY, REALLY SPECIAL. IF YOU KNOW WHAT I MEAN! BUT YOU KNOW WHAT? I WAS THE ONE THAT WAS SUPRISED! SO TELL ME THIS, SMOKIE...IF HE WON'T MESS AROUND ON ME, HOW IS IT THAT I CAUGHT HIM IN BED WITH SOMEBODY ELSE?"

For a few seconds there was silence. I sat there with my mouth open because I could not believe what I had just screamed. I couldn't even hear Smokie breathing. I sighed and closed my eyes.

Smokie finally spoke, a little softer and a little slower then before, "Shelby, uhm...I, uhm, this is... this is deep! I can't tell you what you saw or what you thought you saw, but I know uhm, Julian loves you and he wouldn't do anything to hurt you or mess up what he's got with you. He has never told me about being with anybody else since he met you. I can't tell you what you saw, but I think you should uhm, talk with him."

What was I supposed to say? The conversation was over! I caught him in a lie and he was stumped, speechless! All I could say was, "Good night Smokie."

He blew out a breath and said, "Good night..."

As I hung up the phone I heard him say, "Deg!"

CHAPTER
17

Not a day went by after the awards show that
Kyme or Tracie didn't try to convince me to call Julian. I
never told them about the conversation that I had with
Smokie. I was still a little bothered by it and honestly, I had
expected to hear from Julian by now.   Sharrin called me
about a week after my conversation with Smokie. She told
me that Smokie had called her back that same night after he
got off of the phone with me. She claimed he was very
upset and for once in his life he was at a loss for
words...speechless! But it wasn't because of what I
thought. She told me that she had promised him that she
wouldn't talk to me about it, so she would only say that she
thought I should talk with Julian because it's possible that
things weren't exactly as they seemed. I asked her what she
meant by that, but she wouldn't tell me anything else
because she said she had promised Smokie. A couple of
times I was tempted to call Julian. I picked up the phone to
call, but each time I got a sick feeling in the pit of my stomach, like I was going to throw up, so I hung up.
  On a Friday, about two weeks after my conversation

with Smokie, I was about to call it a day at work. I was clearing off my desk when the phone rang.

"Denval Senior High, this is Ms. Simone."

For a brief moment there was silence. So I said it again, "Denval High, this is Ms. Simone."

The voice on the other end sounded sweetly familiar. I swear if I didn't know any better, I think my heart actually stopped beating.

"Hi Shelby, this is Julian. Please don't hang up."

I said okay, so he continued to talk.

"I uhm, can't remember what I was going to say. It's good to hear your voice though. Look, I called because I want to see you. I know we have some unresolved issues. I would like an opportunity to talk with you about everything. I understand that you don't want to see me right now, but it would mean a lot to me if you would agree to meet me tomorrow night? Before you answer I just want you to know that I won't call you any more if that's what you really want. I'll accept that it's over, but it would mean a lot to me if you would meet me for dinner. Maybe for what might be the last time that we'll ever see each other."

Just hearing his voice made my eyes fill with tears. I really did want to see him and he was right, it probably would be the last time that we would see each other, so I agreed to meet him.

"Where do you want to meet?"

I could feel his smile through the telephone, so I smiled too.

"Mr. Vestas will pick you up right after sunset, around 8:30pm or 9:00pm. I can't wait to see you baby...thank you. I'll see you tomorrow night."

I said bye and we hung up.

Instead of rushing home and calling Kyme and Tracie, I headed for the Galleria to get a new outfit. If this was going to be the last time that we saw each other I wanted to be "drop dead" gorgeous. I wanted Julian to see what he was losing. I wonder if men do that, try to make themselves look extra good to someone they've broken up with. It sort of makes the breakup bittersweet and hopefully makes the other person sorry that they broke up with you. I didn't stay in the mall long. I knew what I wanted, so I went in, looked for it, bought it, and then left. After I found my, "you gonna' be sorry you cheated on me outfit," I grabbed me a bite to eat and headed home. Once I got home I realized that I was too nervous to eat, so I tried to relax by taking a bath. My bath relaxed me, but I couldn't go to sleep, so I watched music videos. Wouldn't you know it, one of Julian's videos came on. I smiled, turned the TV off, and went to bed.

The next day seemed to drag on and on. Kyme and Tracie each had things to do, which was good for me because I didn't feel like hanging out anyway. I called my parents and talked with them for about an hour and I did a three-way call with my brothers and sisters. Talking with my family always puts me at ease. After getting off of the phone with them I felt ready to face the world. The limousine arrived to pick me up right after the sunset, but of course in Shelby style I wasn't ready! When I stood in front of the mirror I looked at myself from head to toe and thought, "I'm not going to cry tonight! I'm not going to cry!" I headed for the limo before I changed by mind. Once I sat down in the car the driver, Mr. Vestas, and I struck up a conversation. I hadn't seen him in a while and of course that was one of the first questions he asked me.

"Good to see you Shelby! Where have you been, I haven't seen you in a while? You know I told Julian that I liked you when I first met you! That young man seems to have a good head on his shoulders, but he's still young. When I missed you coming around I pulled him to the side one day and told him he better not let you get away because you were a "keeper!" I'm not saying he's had a lot of women. I'm just saying out of his few female friends that I've met, you have had more respect about yourself then any of them! I mean that! Look at you, you're just beautiful! That boy better not act crazy, that's all I got to say...he better not act crazy!"

I smiled and looked out the car window. I thanked Mr. Vestas. "You're too kind Mr. Vestas. You must have known that I needed to hear that."

Mr. Vestas, always quick to respond, "Uh, uh I didn't know that, but it makes me feel good to tell the truth...sure do."

When I asked where we were going Mr. Vestas would-n't tell me. Instead, he told me not to ask him again because it was a surprise. Now "that" sparked my curiosity because I couldn't even begin to figure out where we were going. I knew that it would be some place romantic. Well, actually I didn't know that! Maybe it would be some place that had a lot of people and space because we hadn't seen each other in months and Julian probably didn't want to appear to forward or anxious. Then again, maybe he chose a quaint little secluded place, so we could talk with no interruptions. While I was trying to figure out where I was being taken, we pulled into the driveway of the Victorial

Botanical Gardens. I still couldn't figure out what was going on. We drove all the way to the back of the property to the estate mansion, where Mr. Vestas proceeded to pull around to the side and park. At this point I was truly baffled, I couldn't imagine why we were meeting here.

Mr. Vestas proceeded to exit the car and come around to open my door.

I thanked him and asked, "Where's Julian?"

He told me to go down the walk, that was a few feet in front of me, and go through the gate.

He continued, "Once you go through the gate you should find your way all right."

Then he escorted me across the grass to the sidewalk.

"You have a good night, okay?"

I looked at him and said, "Okay..."

As soon as I got to the gate I could see candles going down both sides of the walkway. When I walked through the gate it was breath taking! I reminded myself,

"Remember, you're not going to cry." I took a deep breath and continued to walk. I never would have imagined this. I already felt like I was going to give into whatever he said, but I wasn't going into this night blindly. I had taken a lot of time to think and I decided that, in part, everybody was right. I did need to listen to Julian's side. Like Kyme said, I shouldn't base my decision on the things that happened to me in my marriage. That was a different time, a different place, and definitely a different man. The situation and the circumstances were all different. I needed to base my decision on the history that Julian and I had created, not the history that I had with my ex. I was going into this night completely objective...and totally emotional.

When I got to the end of the walk I could see a table set for two, with a single lit candle as a centerpiece. The table was sitting in the middle of a gazebo that was covered with some kind of flowering vine. I must have gotten there a little faster then Julian had expected because he was straightening his tie and patting his jacket down. He looked sort of like a nervous high school boy waiting for his prom date to come into the room. My goodness, he looked good! Wouldn't you know it, our outfits complimented each other. He had on a brown suit, white shirt and a brown, beige, gold, and white tie. My dress was a silk, off-white tank dress with a dress length sheer jacket that had gold overtones. The jacket had oversized, silk cuffs with gold buttons on each cuff, a silk sash, and a large silk collar with one gold collar button. My shoes were gold sling-backs and my hose were sheer with gold flecks in them. When Julian finally looked up at me it felt like we stood there forever looking at each other. After he came to his senses he started walking towards me. He grabbed me and hugged me. I closed my eyes and held on, that was all I could do at the moment.

While he was holding me, he whispered in my ear, "Thank you for coming Shelby."

When he released his grip he stepped back and told me how beautiful I was.

Once we sat down we had a glass of wine and about 10-15 minutes later dinner was served. I can't remember what we had for dinner, but I remember dessert. After the waiter removed the plates from the table Julian reached across the table and cupped my hands, which I had folded on the table. For the previous 45 minutes or so we had not even discussed the incident with me finding him in bed with another woman. Our dinner discussion was sort of like a "catch up" conversation, so it was about time for him to plead his case.

Julian took my hands and put them up to his lips and kissed them softly. With his eyes closed and his head slightly bowed down he began to speak.

"Shelby, you know I love you. I love you more now then I did before because now I know what it feels like to lose you. You told me once that I never had to swear to you because my word would always be enough."

At this point he opened his eyes and he looked at me.

"You have my word. I would never do anything to

hurt you. I would rather hurt myself first. Smokie told me what you saw. I'm telling you Shelby, that night that you walked into my bedroom and caught me in bed with another woman...nothing had happened, nothing was going to happen! That night I walked into my room, got undressed, and got straight into bed. The next thing I knew Camilla was crawling on top of me, and that must have been when you opened the door. I know it's hard to believe, but that's what happened. By the time I wrestled her off I guess you were gone.

I tried to call you the next morning and for weeks after that, but you would never answer your phone and you never returned any of my calls. I even tried coming by your place and your job, but you were never there. For the last couple of months I've been trying to figure out what happened with us and how I could get you back. This is the best that I could do. I love you."

I know I said I wasn't going to cry and I hadn't, but I did have tears in my eyes. I don't know if that was because of what he'd just said or if it was because he had tears in his eyes. Julian looked so beautiful to me at that moment that I wanted to apologize to him for all of the time that I had wasted. He wasn't finished yet though.

"Shelby, for me tonight has to be all or nothing. I know that if I do nothing I lose you forever, so the choice for me was easy. I have to play my hand."

He let my hands go, reached into his jacket pocket, and pulled out a small jewelry box. When he opened it I saw the biggest marquis diamond that I had ever seen in my life! The ring was platinum and gold and the stone had to be about seven or eight carats, with four one to two-carat side diamonds. It was like something a girl could only dream of. It was beautiful and it sparkled in the candlelight. If I remember correctly, I stopped breathing and started crying. I think it was only when he started talking again that I actually started breathing.

"I want you to be my wife Shelby. I need to know that I will always have you in my life. I want you to be my best friend, my lover, my wife, the mother of my children, and anything else you think you might want to be. Will you have me? Will you marry me?"

I really don't remember saying yes, but I guess I did. I do remember us standing there crying and holding each other. We talked for the next two to three hours. We decided that we would see each other the next evening and start working on our wedding plans. Julian wanted to get married as soon as possible. He said he didn't want to waste any more time.

Julian walked me to the limo and kissed me good night like I was a princess. As I sat in the back of the limo I was besides myself. Mr. Vestas asked if we were going to be all right? I showed him my hand and told him that we were going to get married.

Mr. Vestas said, "I knew that boy wasn't crazy! Congratulations! I told Gladys I'd dance at your wedding one day. Congratulations!"

I called Tracie from the car phone,   "Tracie, I'm coming over. Call Kyme I have something I want to tell both of y'all."

I knew I had woke Tracie up because she sounded kind of crazy and because it was about 2:00am.

"What?   I mean what?   Is everything all right? Where's Kyme?"

By the time I hung up the phone I had decided that I'd call Kyme myself, and she could call Tracie on three-way. Of course, Kyme asked me a thousand questions, one of which was, why was I up at this time of night calling people? I didn't have time to answer any questions and besides, I wanted to tell them at the same time that Julian Brishard and I were getting married!"

CHAPTER
18

The next few weeks were absolutely mind blowing! Julian suggested having the wedding and the reception at his house, that way our parents and other family members could just stay at his house after the festivities were over. We met with the florist and the wedding coordinator several times to discuss the kind of flowers we wanted and where we wanted them placed throughout the house and the yard. We decided on a six layer, yellow and chocolate, white icing cake, with lilies and various colored tulips and greenery cascading down it. The tuxedos would be black and the cummerbunds would be multi-colored (black, white, blue, silver, and fuchsia). The bride's maids dresses were periwinkle blue. For the reception there would be sixty tent-covered tables, with table settings for eight. We decided on putting strings of little white lights on the ceiling of the tents. We thought that would make the backyard very cozy and romantic. The place settings that we selected were white with a platinum and gray-banded pattern. The wineglasses and the water goblets were crystal and the flatware was sterling silver. The centerpieces on the tables would be white and light blue flowers and white candles. We would also have candles placed throughout the yard and the house because the wedding would be at sunset. The food for the reception would be catered because Miss Gladys would be a guest, as well as Mr. Vestas and Miss Bracie (the housekeeper). Julian and I worked on the menu with the caterer. There would be three open bars, one in the house and two outside and the food would be served buffet style. Oh yea, we also had a gazebo built. Julian and I worked on the seating and table arrangements. We decided to place two hundred chairs around the gazebo and to take our vows under the gazebo (anybody that didn't get there on time could stand up through the reading of the vows). We also agreed that flower petals and floating candles in the pool would add a special touch. Julian was a doll! He helped with everything except my dress and the dresses for the bride's maids and our mothers.

It goes without saying that my girls, Tracie and Kyme were with me helping out every step of the way. We giggled like teenage girls when we were together talking about the wedding. They helped me pick out my gown, which I wanted to be very simple, but beautiful and the bride's maid dresses because they would be wearing them. The gown I eventually selected for myself was white with pearl and silver crystal beading. It had hand tatted German lace that fit off the shoulder. It was long sleeved with small, pearl buttons down the front, and a four-foot train down the back.

Underneath the lace was a spaghetti strapped, white silk satin dress with a low cut back. My shoes were two and a half-inch white, satin sling-backs. At one point when I was trying on dresses I started crying. Kyme walked up behind me and put her arms around me.

"You okay?"

I shook my head, "Yea, for a minute I got a little overwhelmed with everything. Kyme, I can't believe this, everything is happening so fast. I was just standing here looking at myself in the mirror thinking that I can't believe I'm getting married...in just a few days? I know I'm being a little silly, but for a minute I had a head rush!"

Kyme was still standing behind me when she hugged me.

"Everything is going to be all right! You're just nervous, like any one of us would be if we were in your place. You're going to be a beautiful bride, you're going to have a beautiful wedding, and you're going to live happily ever after. You've found everybody's' dream man and you know that you both love each other and that didn't happen over night. It actually took y'all a good little while to get to this point. I know that you're both going to work very hard at keeping each other happy and making this marriage work."

We left the dress shop that day with wedding gown and tiara in hand.

On the day of the wedding I was surprised at how nervous I was. My mom, my sisters, and my best friends were there, but I was a mess. It was still hard for me to

believe that Julian and I had made it this far. Just a month
ago I was sure that it was over and I would never see him
again. If it hadn't been for that phone call from Smokie I
would still be thinking that Julian cheated on me. It's amazing how I misinterpreted the whole situation. I guess the
saying, "Believe none of what you hear and half of what you
see," does apply sometimes. In just a few short hours I
would be Mrs. Julian "Jules" Brishard! Wow, it was unbelievable...then I heard my mom's voice.

"What are you thinking about? Didn't you hear us
come into the room?"

I looked up at her and Julian's mom and smiled. Miss
Brishard looked at me and started laughing.

"Are you having second thoughts?"

My mother responded, "She can't be any more nervous
then I am. I've never been to a wedding with so many
celebrities. I feel like I'm getting married."

We all laughed and hugged as Tracie, Kyme, Kari, and
Sharrin came into the room to help me get dressed. They
were so pretty that it brought tears to my eyes. We had all
gotten our hair and nails done that morning (including my
mother, Julian's mom, and his grandmother). This was my
way of showing them my appreciation for sharing this special day with Julian and me. We also bought a pair of 1/2-
carat diamond earrings, as well as a small diamond and sap-
phire necklace for everyone in the wedding party. We
bought the guys really nice silver and diamond cufflinks.

After I put my dress on I stood in the mirror and

looked at myself. The first time I was married I didn't have a wedding, so this was especially emotional for me. As everyone fussed over me I thought about what Julian said the first time we went to a party together, "You're going to be the center of attention, but don't worry, I'm going to be right here with you." It was almost time for me to go downstairs, so I took a deep breath and asked Kari if I looked okay. She gave me a hug and said, "You're beautiful." When I walked out the door my niece, who was the flower girl, was sitting on the floor in the hallway outside the room. She was so cute that I laughed out loud. Her dress was a small version of mine. On the floor next to her was her basket filled with blue and white flower petals. She looked up at me.

"Auntie Shell you look pretty!"

I said, "Thank you baby," and grabbed her by her hand. As we all headed for the staircase I thought, "Okay, here we go!"

By the time we got to the door I could see that our mothers had been seated and I could see Julian standing up front looking "faune!" He was stretching his neck to look down the aisle to see if he could see me. I smiled because he looked so anxious, like a teenage boy going on his first date. My dad walked up next to me and grabbed my arm and placed it under his.

He looked at me with tears in his eyes and said, "You look too beautiful to give away baby girl," then he kissed me on my forehead.

I guess this was it. The bride's song to the groom began to play, "I Love You" by Angel Grant. I had to take a couple of deep breaths because my eyes began to tear up. Each bride's maid was met at the door by her groomsman and escorted down the aisle and then Kari and her husband headed down the aisle, then Sharrin and Smokie. The ring bearer, one of my nephews, went out, but not without some coaxing. It appeared that at the last minute he changed his mind and decided he wanted to sit down and watch the wedding.

My niece looked up at my dad and me and said, "Auntie Shell and Pappa I'm not going to cry because I'm a big girl!"

My dad looked at her and said, "I know, you're Pappa's big girl!"

She smiled and headed down the aisle gently throwing flower petals to each side of the aisle. When she reached the front "The Wedding March" began to play and everyone stood up. I looked up at my dad, he smiled and patted my hand that was holding on to his forearm and we began to slowly walk down the aisle. It seemed like I was moving in slow motion. The whole scene felt surreal. I looked up at Julian, he wasn't smiling, he had a sort of funny look on his face (he later told me it was because he couldn't believe how beautiful I looked coming down the aisle).

When we reached the front Julian gently took my hand to lead me up the stairs of the gazebo. My father kissed me on my cheek, stepped back and took his seat. The minister, David, was a friend of mine, he asked everyone to bow their heads so we could pray.

"Who gives this woman to this man?"

My father proudly stood up from his seat and said, in a slightly shaky voice, "Her mother and I do," and then he sat back down.

Julian looked at him as if to say, "Yea..."

David read some scriptures from the bible, sharing with us the role of a husband and a wife. He talked about being fair and loving, having realistic expectations of each other. One thing that he said that I really appreciated was that we hadn't done all of this hard work and planning for just one day, but that hopefully we had done all of this hard work and planning to prepare for a life together. He also read some scriptures from the bible about love, then he began with the wedding vows. After I said my vows I began to put Julian's ring on his finger. I thought I was going to drop it because my hands were shaking so badly. When Julian said his vows they were strong and certain. How could I have ever doubted this man's love for me? I was shaking even more when he started putting my ring on my finger. I actually thought I was going to pass out! Julian softly reassured me that it was going to be all right. After he slid the ring on my finger I looked up at him with tears in my eyes. I couldn't believe that we had finally done it, we were married. So, I wondered what was taking the minister so long to say, "I now pronounce you husband and wife?" I had no idea what was going on because this should have been the end of the wedding according to the program. I

looked at Julian kind of baffled like, "What's going on?"
Smokie reached into his pocket and handed Julian a cordless
microphone. Julian grinned and began to sing:

> You are the breath that I breathe
> Your love makes me pray
> for more then 24 hours in a day
>
> Everytime I close my eyes
> I dream dreams of fantasies
> You, me
> Us, we
> lifc, love,
> so long, forever
> together, together, together
>
> I promise you love
> that none can compare
> and happiness brand new
>
> Thank you for teaching me,
> showing me
> love's seed
> planted
> watered
> grown
> bloomed
> to a forever us,

a forever we
a forever love

Everytime I close my eyes
I dream dreams of fantasies
You, me
Us, we
life, love,
so long, forever
together, together, together

You are my sweet lady,
my sweet baby,
my honey,
my boo

Each day will begin and end with you
me
we
us
together, forever, forever, forever
(ain't no end to what our love will do)

Everytime I close my eyes
I dream dreams of fantasies
you, me
us, we
life, love,

so long, forever
together, together, together

As hard as I tried not to, I couldn't stop myself, I started crying. Julian had written a song for our wedding, "Every Time I Close My Eyes." He was unbelievable! I hoped this was a small indication of how the rest of our life together was going to be. Even though I didn't think it was even possible to love him more then I did at that moment. When he finished singing David said, "I now pronounce you husband and wife. You may now kiss the bride!"

Everybody started clapping and Julian gently placed his hands on either side of my face and said, "I love you Shelby." We kissed, finally... husband and wife.

There was really no where to exit to, so we walked into the house and then went back outside for pictures. After the photographer finished taking pictures we made a receiving line to give everyone at the wedding an opportunity to meet the wedding party and for Julian and I to introduce ourselves as husband and wife. That sounded sort of freaky to me. Julian and I were now "husband and wife." What was even freakier was that we had the nerve to think that we were going to shake hands with over four hundred guests...I don't think so! This also gave the yard crew the opportunity to move the chairs around. The wedding party's table was going to be on the gazebo, so that we could see and be seen by everybody at the reception. Half way through shaking hands someone handed Julian a microphone. He announced to our guests that we were going to take our seats so that we could begin eating. For those who had not had an opportunity to come through the line, Julian suggested perhaps coming up to our table or meeting us as we mingled later. My man, taking control of the situation.

All of the tables were numbered so the guests could find their tables based on the number that was on their invitations. We thought it was fair to randomly place numbers on all of the invitations. The buffet line went quickly. Of course the wedding party was served first. I got just a little something because I really wasn't very hungry and neither was Julian. If it wasn't for the fact that we are both right handed, we would have held hands throughout dinner, but it was physically impossible to eat and hold hands at the same time.

Julian wouldn't tell me where we were going for our honeymoon, so all during the reception I kept whispering in his ear asking, "Where are we going? Come on, tell me."

He would look at me and smile and say, "It's a surprise! Stop asking me because I'm not gonna' tell you."

Even though I spent the entire reception in suspense, it was great! Not only did I still feel the butterflies from just having become Mrs. Julian Brishard, but I also felt an explosive anticipation of what was to come later. My Dad and I danced the first dance. While we were dancing my Dad whispered in my ear.

"I told Julian that he better take care of you."

He smiled and I smiled back.

My Dad then said, "Really, I want y'all to take care of each other, okay?" and he kissed me on the cheek.

As tears rolled down my cheek I shook my head okay. My Dad then led me by my hand over to Julian. Julian and I danced to LTD's Love Ballad. As the music played Julian sang to me, "I have never been so much/In love/Before/What a difference/A true love made in my life/So nice/So right/ Lovin you gave me somethin new/That I've never felt/Never dreamed of/Something's changed/Though it's not the/Feeling I had before/Oh, it's much, much more..." He held me so tightly that I got the feeling that he was never going to let me go again. It was a pretty nice feeling.

I would have been satisfied with staying at Julian's house and kicking everybody else out at the end of the night, but it was Julian's idea to make our wedding as convenient as possible for our family and friends. It was the perfect place for a wedding, a wedding reception, and a hotel. The plan was that some time during the reception, Julian and I were going to sneak out and drive to the airport to catch a flight to who knows where and in the mean time our families would stay at the house and relax. Julian had a master plan and he had thought every step through. For a wedding gift he gave me $8,000 to go shopping for a new wardrobe to wear during the honeymoon. He gave me very explicit instructions about how I was to spend the money. It was to be spent for clothes, shoes, lingerie and anything else that I needed for a honeymoon in warm weather and not on anything for the wedding or on a gift for him. Kyme, Tracie, and I had a great time shopping for two weeks worth of warm weather clothes and stuff. I didn't really need to buy any lingerie because I had received enough during the bridal shower to last an entire month. It was going to be fun trying to wear it all.

It was kind of nice seeing Smokie and Sharrin together. They made a really cute couple. I think they're good for each other. For whatever reason, they seem to have a calming effect on one another. Smokie and I had sure come a long way. I didn't dislike him any more, as a matter of fact, I was rather fond of him. Miss Gladys told me a long time ago that he was a nice boy and I guess she was right. If it hadn't been for Smokie, Julian and I probably would have never spoken to each other again. That would have been a really sad way to end things, but instead here we are at our wedding reception. Speaking of which, as I looked around the yard it was beautiful. The tent covered tables, the centerpieces of candles, white tulips, periwinkle blue iris, and other flowers. The bridesmaids were absolutely beautiful in their silk satin, periwinkle blue, spaghetti strapped dresses and silk organza wraps with satin trim. It all looked like a scene from a dream.

My sisters where absolutely gorgeous, they were my maid and matron of honor. My brothers were also a part of the wedding party. Poor CoCo was going to kill himself trying to dance with every single woman at the reception. That boy worried me...looking for a woman, but looking at all the wrong things! Julian's and my parents were sitting and talking. It was good to see them all getting along so well. Julian's mom and grandmom were going to spend their next vacation at my parents' home. That should be interesting. Anyway...the guests seemed to be having a good time. I continued to look around and I saw Julian across the yard. He winked at me and smiled. My baby is just too sweet and good looking for words. He looked just as good to me on our wedding day as he did the first day we met. I almost started crying as I stood there looking at him. I loved him so much...my husband.

For the entire reception I kept waiting for Julian to sneak up behind me and grab my hand, so that we could make a quick get away to the airport, but it never happened. The wedding started at 8:30pm and was finished by 9:15pm. The reception started immediately after the wedding, so I thought that around 11:30pm or 12:00am we would disappear and leave everyone partying, but it never happened. At 11:00pm we cut the cake and I thought for sure we would sneak out after that...didn't happen! At 11:30pm Julian and I danced, so I knew that after that we would leave. Julian held me as we danced and whispered in my ear. "Are you tired?" I smiled at him and said, "Are you?" Julian kind of stood back and looked at me, as he shook his head and said, "Uh, huh!" So I thought, "Oh good, this must be the cue to leave, but instead we kept right on dancing. Smokie stepped in and he and I danced for a while. He told me I was a beautiful bride. I said thanks.

Smokie continued, "I've never seen Jules this happy and I know it's because of you. I want this one day too..."

I looked at him and said, "What, a big wedding?"

He laughed and said, "No. I mean what y'all have...when y'all look at each other everybody can see that you love each other. Even when y'all are near other people they can feel your love. That's what I want! People can live off of what y'all have leftover. It's a trip!"

I told Smokie he could have the same thing, but it meant showing what he had inside. He knew that though. I gave Smokie a hug and kissed him on the cheek and said, "You'll find it, watch and see." When Smokie and I finished dancing Julian and I sat down at our table. Different people walked up to talk with us and to congratulate us. While we were sitting there our parents walked over to give us more hugs and to say goodnight. At midnight I was too tired to even care about leaving and frankly a little irked that we were still at the reception! I knew that our luggage had been in the car all day and all I could think about now was getting out of my dress and going to sleep.

Julian looked at me and kissed me on my cheek. He smiled and said, "Give me your hand."

He reached for my hand, but I said, "Uh, uh...I don't want to dance anymore."

He grabbed my hand, "Just let me hold your hand girl." He had to pull me to my feet because I wasn't going to get up. He led me through the crowd into the house.

When we got to the staircase I asked, "Where are we

going Julian?"

Julian didn't utter a word as he led me upstairs to his bedroom. When he opened the door the room had been filled with candles, the bed had been turned back, and one of my new nighties was on the bed.

I looked at Julian and said, "What's going on?" Julian locked the door and said, "You looked tired. I thought you might want to go to bed." I was confused because I had been expecting to leave all night and instead we were still at the house, in Julian's bedroom. "So, we're not going anywhere?"

Julian gave me a kiss and said, "I'll wake you up when it's time to go."

I was too tired to ask any more questions, so I put on my nightie and went to bed. Julian held me in his arms and we both fell asleep. I guess he was tired too.

CHAPTER
19

*T*he next morning Julian woke me up, "Wake up Shell, it's time to go."

I rolled over on my stomach and whined, "What time is it?"

Julian laughed as he pulled me out of the bed, "Come on girl, you don't want to miss the plane do you?"

I got up even though I wanted to sleep for at least another four hours. When I looked at the clock I realized why I wanted to sleep longer, it was only 4:00am. I drug myself into the shower, brushed my teeth, and found some clothes to put on. Someone had graciously taken a sundress out of my suitcase for me. It must have been Kari, but that was okay because I planned to get them all later. I'm pretty sure everybody knew what was going on, but agreed not to tell me anything. We got into the limo at exactly 4:45am. I laid my head on Julian's shoulder and fell back asleep. I was too sleepy to ask where we were flying off to.

When we got to the airport Julian woke me up and we walked straight to the gate. I realized later that he had sent our luggage ahead. When we reached the gate I noticed that the flight board said Miami, Fl, so I figured we were headed for Miami. I still didn't ask any questions because if we were going to spend our honeymoon in Coconut Grove that was cool with me. It was a 6:37am flight and frankly, I still wasn't in the mood to hold a conversation. When we changed planes in Miami I was a little more alert. Julian and I held hands as we walked through the airport to our next flight. Because it was still relatively early, there weren't a lot of people in the airport stopping Julian for his autograph. He was relieved because he was concerned about the fanfare. He knew that it could be quite intimidating to constantly be approached for autographs and the like, so he planned the flights early in the morning to keep me from being overwhelmed. My baby, always thinking on his feet. I eventually figured out that our destination was the West Indies, but I wasn't sure which island.

On our flight to the West Indies Julian and I talked about how well both the wedding and the reception went. We were both anxious to see the wedding pictures when we returned to the States. Neither one of us could believe everything that had transpired in the last few months.

Julian looked at me and said, "You know, I knew I had to marry you because I couldn't stop thinking about you when I couldn't find you. I thought for sure that you had found somebody else." He paused, "I missed you so much. I knew, I just knew."

I put my hand up to his lips, "I missed you too and I promise you that won't ever happen again...ever."

We kissed and then talked until the plane landed in St. Lucia at the Hewanorra Airport. We rented a Range Rover at the airport and drove to Petit Piton. Julian still wouldn't tell me exactly where we were going, so I anxiously rode to our destination. The jungle terrain we rode through was beautiful. Julian reminded me of a conversation that we had early in our relationship. At the time we were still meeting at the restaurant for dinner. One night he asked me where I'd go if I just wanted to get away from everything to relax. I told him that I would go to an island and hide away in an open-air cottage that overlooked an ocean.

I looked at him and said, "You remember me telling you that?"

He laughed and said, "Girl, I remember everything you've ever said to me."

I saw several estates while we were riding. I thought that for sure we'd stop at one of them. We rode until we came to a beautiful white cottage with orange shutters, surrounded by all kinds of tropical flowers. Julian practically rode up to the front door and stopped. When I got out of the car and walked toward the cottage I could see that it overlooked the Caribbean Sea. I couldn't believe that Julian had done this because of a conversation we had when we first met. I shook my head in disbelief and, of course, I started crying.

Julian walked up to me and put his arms around me, "Are you all right baby?"

I turned around and kissed him, "This is unbelievable,

I can't believe you were able to do this. I can't believe you remembered something I told you so long ago. Thank you…"

Julian looked at me and said, "Anything for you!"

We held hands as we went into the house. It was so cute. There was an open living room, a large kitchen, and beautiful live flower arrangements throughout the house. Adjacent to the kitchen was a veranda with a dining table on one side and a large hammock on the other side. Down the stairs from the veranda was a large pool. The master bedroom had a king sized four poster bed and French doors that opened up to a terrace. There was also a huge ensuite bathroom. The furniture in the cottage was gorgeous. Julian told me that we were near a volcano, several botanical gardens, a few mineral baths, and a beach. I was still in awe that he had gone through such great lengths to make our honeymoon so special.

While we were standing in the doorway between the veranda and the kitchen, I looked at Julian and asked, "How did you find this place?"

He took a deep breath, "Well, It really wasn't that difficult. I knew some folks that came to the Caribbean quite regularly, so I asked them if they knew of any places like this on any of the islands. They gave me the name of a realtor, I contacted her, flew down here to check out a few places, and the rest is history.

We didn't have to spend any time unpacking because someone had already done that for us. Julian had arranged to have a cook on call for most of our stay. We weren't that far from the local restaurants, so we could leave the house for meals if we chose too. We were only in the house for about an hour when Julian told me to freshen up because we were going to go out for lunch. I wasn't disappointed, but I was kind of surprised that Julian wanted to leave so soon. We had been together for almost two years and we had never made love and now that we were married I thought for sure he'd get started as quickly as possible. Maybe I was more anxious then him. As we drove to the restaurant I couldn't get over how beautiful the island was. We had a fantastic lunch at the Caribbean Gardens restaurant. During lunch I couldn't stop looking at Julian. He was a phenomenal man...a keeper...a real dream come true.

After lunch we walked around town and did a little sight seeing. By the time we got back to the cottage it was 6:30pm. We walked around a little more outside and looked at the surrounding landscape. I was happier then I had been in years and it wasn't because Julian made me happy as much as it was that I realized I was really in control of my own happiness. I was able to share myself with someone else and trust that he would share himself with me. It was a big relief to have freed myself to give and receive love again. Julian walked up behind me and put his arms around my waist. He asked me what I was thinking about.

I looked at him sort of sideways, "Nothing...I'm just happy to be here...with you!"

He kissed me on my cheek and said, "Come on, let's go

inside."

Before we settled in for the night we wanted to find out where our clothes had been delivered. After Julian finished he jumped in the shower. He came out of the bathroom in a pair of silk, maroon pajama bottoms.

He hopped in the bed and patted it as he asked, "When are you going to come to bed?"

I laughed and said, "I don't know, it's still kind of early. I was thinking that I'd read for a couple of hours and then come to bed."

Julian looked at me and said, "Oh, okay! Wake me up when you come to bed."

Instead of responding I went into the bathroom to take my shower. After my shower I took my time and lotioned my body from head to toe, combed my hair back, and dabbed on just a little bit of perfume. I felt like a virgin on her wedding night, and that made me giggle to myself.

It had been about three years since I had been with Lorenz and months since the last near miss with Julian. I had to tell myself to calm down because it was okay now...we were married. This was how it was supposed to be. I took a deep breath, turned off the bathroom light, and opened the door.

Julian had turned off the lights and lit several candles. I stood in the doorway of the bathroom and looked at him. I loved the way he looked at me. I can't even articulate the way his eyes make me feel.

He sat up on the edge of the bed and said, "Come

here..."

Without breaking my gaze, I slowly walked over to him. As I stood in front of him he placed his hands on my waist and kissed my stomach. Then he laid his head on my belly and held me. His hands moved up my calves to the back of my thighs to the small of my back. I felt chills throughout my entire body. Then he got up and stood behind me. He ran his hands up both of my arms and stopped at my shoulders. I was shaking so much that Julian asked, "Why are you shaking? Are you nervous?" I closed my eyes, bit my bottom lip, and shook my head from side to side. Julian kissed me on both of my shoulders then he kissed either side of my neck. I could feel my straps fall from my shoulders one at a time and then my nightie fell to the floor. Julian's hands were all over my body. It felt so good that I thought I was going to pass out. I kept thinking, "It's finally going to happen." Julian picked me up and laid me on the bed. As we kissed, each of his movements was slow and concise. He gave attention to each and every part of my body. It seemed like we made love for hours. I had never experienced anything so intense, so good! It felt like every nerve in by entire body had been stimulated. When we finished making love we were both covered in sweat and unable to say a word. My mind and my body were totally spent! I lay there quietly in Julian's arms.

Julian pushed my hair out of my face, so he could look at me, "You okay?"

I shook my head and said, "Uh, huh...yea."

We both fell asleep, waking up several times during the night to make love again, and again, and again.

We woke up the next morning to the smell of breakfast. It was kind of weird knowing that someone had been in the house cooking while we were sleeping, but if Julian was comfortable with the arrangement then so was I. We put our robes on, brushed our teeth, washed our faces, and went into the kitchen. I didn't know about Julian, but I would have rather stayed in the bed for a few more hours, and not just to sleep I might add. We found toasted English muffins, scrambled eggs, turkey bacon, fresh fruit, and juice. The cook had placed two place settings, as well as fresh flowers on the table on the veranda. We fixed our plates and had breakfast.

As we were eating I asked Julian, "So what do you have planned for us today?"

Julian looked up from his plate and said, "I don't know about you, but all I want to do today is make love, eat, and sleep!"

I looked at him and said, "Oh, I think I can work that into my schedule."

Julian excused himself from the table and called the company that sent the cook over. He told them that we wanted the cook to come back to prepare dinner around 6:00pm that day, as well as the next day, and that we also wanted her to come by and fix breakfast again the next morning. So it goes without saying that we spent the next couple of days hold up in the cottage making love, eating, sleeping, and then waking up and starting all over again.

We eventually ventured away from the cottage. We walked the beach, visited some of the botanical gardens, and swam in the mineral springs. We took hundreds of pictures to show to our family and friends. Our last morning on the island rolled around so quickly that I asked Julian if we could stay another week.

He laughed and said, "You know, we can do everything we did here at home. Know what I mean?"

He patted my behind and walked out of the room.

As we boarded the stairs of the plane I knew our honeymoon was officially over. When we arrived at the airport in Miami someone recognized Julian. Fortunately, he had scheduled fans into our travel plans this time, so we had more then enough time for him to sign autographs and for us to get from one flight to the next. I guess this was the beginning of our life together and my life as a celebrity's wife.

It was obvious that someone had leaked our return to the press. When we landed at our final destination reporters and fans were everywhere. Women were holding up signs, "We love you Jules!; Congratulations!; We missed you!; I'll wait, I'm really the one for you!" Smokie and Julian's bodyguards got us through the crowd and escorted us to the limo. I couldn't believe how the women were swarming around us. It was sort of intimidating! I asked Julian if it was always like that? He told me that he took the earliest or the latest flights for just that very reason, to avoid crowds as much as possible. Wow, what had I gotten myself into? I hoped that was as bad as it was ever going to get. Julian must have known what I was thinking.

He grabbed my hand and kissed me on the cheek, "You don't have to worry about anything. I'm going to make sure that our life is very private and that you and the kids are always safe."

I looked up at that joker and he was smiling like a Cheshire cat. What "kids" was he talking about?

Well, I wasn't really worried, I knew Julian was going to be a great husband and father. I looked forward to our life together.